Exodus Unwanted

Robert B. Kugel, MD

FIRESIDE FICTION
2006

FIRESIDE FICTION
AN IMPRINT OF HERITAGE BOOKS, INC.

Books, CDs, and more—Worldwide

For our listing of thousands of titles see our website
at
www.HeritageBooks.com

Published 2006 by
HERITAGE BOOKS, INC.
Publishing Division
65 East Main Street
Westminster, Maryland 21157-5026

Other books by the author:

*Victory Without Swords: The Story of Pat and Lily Okura
Japanese American Citizens in 1941 America*

International Standard Book Number: 978-0-7884-4076-4

EXODUS UNWANTED

Dedication

The book is dedicated to the many thousands of immigrants who came from Europe to America seeking a new life. Many came eagerly hoping to find relief from wars, oppression, hunger, and disillusionment. Some came for adventure and opportunity to strike it rich. Others came because they were forced to leave as the result of various altered political circumstances and the social upheaval which followed in the wake of frequent wars.

EXODUS UNWANTED

TABLE OF CONTENTS

PREFACE

Great waves of immigrants from Europe poured into America during the 19th Century. Europe had been in turmoil during much of the century, starting with the Napoleonic Wars, continuing with the mid century 1848 revolutions and ending with the Franco-Prussian war. Upheaval was everywhere from the Scandinavian countries to Italy and from France to Russia.

Many immigrants came with the hope of escaping the ravages of war, avoiding military conscription and evading the drudgery of factory life. Stories of riches to be had in America and abundance of free land were strong inducements.

Some few immigrants who had been prospering in Europe sought asylum after political changes made life in Europe unbearable. This is the story of one such family for whom readjustment was necessary but exceedingly difficult. After a period of time they, too, accommodated to the America of the 19th Century.

CHAPTER 1

The Crisis of Napoleon

Somewhere around his 15th birthday Rudolph had become interested in the events of recent history which he thought had or might have some effect on his life and his way of living. Rudolph was a handsome young man with dark, wavy hair, deep brown eyes, and a ready smile. His manner was polite but not pedantic. Some days he thought his life growing up in a small north German principality was fairly restricted.

It was 1820, five years after the Battle of Waterloo, but Napoleon was still talked about frequently. At the Academy where he was studying, he was perplexed because some of his instructors clearly admired Napoleon while others despised him. Why was this, he thought. One afternoon late in the day, Rudolph decided to seek out his father, Baron von Damsgaard, to help clarify a discussion he had at school. Coming downstairs from his room on the second floor, Rudolph knocked quietly on the door to his father's library.

"Come in," his father said. A most distinguished, austere gentleman, Friedrich, now in his early sixties, was a prominent member of the nobility of Ostend-Aachen, where he had lived all of his life and where his family had lived for over three centuries.

Rudolph entered the library with some trepidation. The library could be forbidding with its book shelves extending from floor to ceiling on the two outer walls. The shelves were crowded with books and papers. He often wondered what they were all about, but that was not a matter for him to consider today.

"Papa, in class the other day, Professor Wannamacher said that the whole of Europe both loved and hated Napoleon. I'm rather confused by that statement. Did we love and hate Napoleon? I can't remember you ever saying you loved Napoleon. What were things like then?" Rudolph asked.

Frederick got up from his desk where he had been reading and came over to the big stove which stood in one corner of the room. Friedrich had dark, serious, kindly eyes. Always well-dressed, he usually wore knee pants, a starched white shirt with a silk neck cloth and a velvet jacket, which

Rudolph thought were old-fashioned.

"First, come, warm your knees over here by the stove and sit down, my boy. It's cold this January," Friedrich said. Rudolph sat down on his favorite chair, a large overstuffed one, in his father's library. He liked the handsome walnut and oak paneled library with its many books, the large globe of the world and his father's huge desk. With a snow storm raging outside, the warmth of the stove was inviting.

"Mind you, the Napoleonic era is quite a story, but some parts I remember all too well. You see, Napoleon affected us in many ways. Let me tell you about one example.

"In the old days His Majesty, the Prince, would periodically call together all of the nobles to inform them of certain decisions which had been made. More often than not he would request funds for various projects. We had such a meeting in 1805, the year you were born. I remember well as you were your mother's first-born.

"You see, the French King, Louis XVI, was long dead and Napoleon had conquered all of France. The Declaration of the Rights of Man, which had been adopted by the French Assembly during the Revolution, was disregarded by Napoleon. It was clear to many of us that Napoleon was hoping to be another Charlemagne and that he would stop at nothing to conquer everything in sight. After he marched into Italy, it was obvious to many of us that he would soon be marching north and east.

"He established what he called the Code of Napoleon, and he imposed its principles throughout all of France and all of the conquered territories in Italy. One of the stipulations was that merchants and other wealthy people would not be required to pay tribute to the lords of the day," Friedrich said.

"I can see where that would not be popular with you," Rudolph said.

"You are absolutely correct. The nobles were violently opposed. You see, after the battle of Marengo in 1800, it looked for a time as though peace would return to all of Europe. However, the peace was like quicksand," Friedrich said.

"What do you mean, it was like quicksand?" Rudolph asked turning his handsome face directly towards his father.

"Well, to begin with, the English and the Russians were terrified. Napoleon had sold the huge Louisiana territory in North America to the United States in 1804 in order to obtain more money for his wars and conquests. Look here at the globe and see how the Louisiana territory almost doubled the land area of the United States," Friedrich said. Rudolph and Friedrich went over to the globe where Friedrich pointed out these new boundaries.

"Then in 1804 he arranged to have the Pope come to Paris to crown him as Emperor. At the ceremony at Notre Dame Cathedral he had the effrontery to crown himself Emperor. The French loved it since it suggested stability and a return to the monarchy. Napoleon was very popular in France, and to a large extent he was popular in the north of Europe as well. He was a man who could get things done. We tend to like people like that. In many ways we Germans have always admired the French and not just because of their good manners.

"The German states were weak when compared with England and Russia, and it was this situation that influenced the Prince to call a special meeting of the nobles in 1805," Friedrich said, glancing at Rudolph, who was paying rapt attention.

"Where was the meeting held, Papa?" Rudolph said.

"It was held in the throne room of the castle. I'm not sure you have ever been in the throne room. It's just above the entry area. We were there almost all day. Since I am the Exchequer, I sat close to the Prince to remind him about the financial impact of various proposals. I knew he was going to talk about a possible union of some of the north German states, which was being discussed, and he would also be talking about new taxes, which would be very unpopular," Friedrich said.

"But wasn't Frederick Wilhelm of Prussia already suggesting some type of union of the north German states?" Rudolph asked.

"Yes he was, but the threat to us was more from France since Napoleon had a huge army and a lot of money. Prussia was a great distance from Ostend-Aachen and, besides, the Prussian army was small in comparison to Napoleon's," Friedrich said.

"So what happened?" Rudolph asked. He was now sitting on the edge of his chair.

"The Prince raised the question of joining a league of north German states, but almost everyone, myself included, wanted no part of it. Then the Prince alluded to other conquests and predicted that Napoleon would sweep across Europe, and we, as a small state, would be pulled into some kind of federation under the domination of the French. He stressed that we would all have to provide more money, which we knew would ultimately find its way to Paris. If we were to remain somewhat independent, we would have to send troops and money to Paris," Friedrich said.

Just then there was a knock at the door.

"Come in," Frederick said.

Magdalene, Rudolph's mother, opened the door and said, "Is this a private conversation or may I join you?"

"Join us by all means, my dear, and sit beside me here on the sofa. Rudolph has been asking about Napoleon, and you might tell him how things looked to you in 1805," Friedrich said.

Magdalene, a beautiful lady in her late thirties, was radiant, dressed in a blue brocade dress. She entered, pulling a large white wool shawl over her shoulders and seated herself next to her husband on the sofa. "Of course, I love to talk about those days," Magdalene said.

"I remember May of that year. I really didn't care a fig about Napoleon or the whole Grand Armee. You see, my son, men and women tend to look at things differently. You had just come into this world, and my attention was almost totally directed to how you and your two older brothers were going to get along.

"Rudolph, I remember sitting in my room one morning in early May, day dreaming. It was a particularly beautiful day, and I kept thinking, was it always so beautiful? And you were as beautiful as the day, my dear.

"I had called Stephanie to come into the room to plan some social activities," Magdalene said.

"Stephanie was then a young woman, about 20, from the village. She had joined the staff five years earlier. She learned quickly so I advanced her to the position of upstairs maid, a position she has now held for, let's see, 17 years. She was a joy to have around. With unfailing accuracy she knew almost exactly what I would want when I rang for her

"Oh, that day in May! How well I remember looking at that section of the garden which is close to the house and is protected from the winds that so often sweep across upper Saxony in the springtime. Already many shoots from the early plantings in the gardens were beginning to show. We were planning a dinner for Maria Josephine, our dowager aunt, who was due to arrive for her spring visit. Later, your   Uncle Philip and Aunt Rosalinde would be coming for a visit," Magdalene said.

"I knew your father and Uncle Philip would want to do some hunting, and afterwards they would do some talking. They were so serious about all the affairs of state which didn't interest me at all. I'd try to get their attention away from the affairs of state.

"I love teasing your father when he gets so serious. I'd say something like, my darling, you look worried, but let me tell you that your son is quite well and even now sleeps peacefully on his nursery cot.

"But your father and Uncle Philip talked on and on about old Napoleon and what the Prince had said. I never knew whether you pronounced his name Napoleone or Napoleon. You see how we see things differently?" Magdalene said as she glanced first towards Rudolph and then to Friedrich.

"Yes, I do," Rudolph said , but his voice didn't sound convincing to himself and probably was not to either of his parents.

"It was probably on just such a morning that I learned about how the French were again massing their forces under Napoleon," Friedrich continued. "We learned that he had gained the crown of Lombardy and was pressing on to Genoa. From there we expected he would move on to the Papal states and the Kingdom of Naples. His Highness said that we would have to join with Austria and Prussia if we were to avoid being eaten alive by the French.""What a state of affairs! Does His Highness think we shall have to send men to Napoleon's army or just tribute to Paris? I asked." Magdalene said.

"Good for you!" Rudolph said, turning towards his mother and giving her one of his wonderful smiles.

"We were happy that our new son was too young to have to put on anyone's uniform," Friedrich said and tousled Rudolph's hair for emphasis.

"As events proceeded, the warning was wise indeed. Napoleon did not stop. He moved on to Vienna in November of 1805, and his march with the Grand Armee across Europe could not be deterred. The French suffered a defeat when Villeneuve was lost to Lord Nelson at the naval Battle of Trafalgar. By December Napoleon had recouped with a major victory at Austerlitz. This was a great victory and restored French confidence in their emperor.

"With the help of old Talleyrand, who was the French Secretary for Foreign Affairs, the map of Europe was soon to be greatly altered. Come over here to the globe and let me show you."

Both Rudolph and Magdalene walked over to the globe. Friedrich began pointing to the various areas of northern Europe which he had been discussing.

"Both Bavaria and Wuertemberg had their territories enlarged and Baden became a duchy, closely allied to France. By 1806 Napoleon had control of the kingdoms of Baden Saxony, Wuertemberg, and Wesphalia, the grand duchies of Anhalt, Oldenburg, Saxe-Coburg, Saxe-Gotha, Saxe-Weimar and many other of the principalities, one of which was Ostend-Aachen. All of this was without precedent in Europe.

"We were shocked to learn later that the Emperor was building a triumphal arch in Paris, called the Arc de Triomphe de l'Etoile, so that all of his soldiers could march up the Champs-Elysees just as the Caesars did in ancient Rome," Friedrich said.

"So far you've not told me much about why we should like Napoleon, let alone love him," Rudolph said.

"No, but we'll come to that. Indeed, I later heard from the Chamberlain that the Emperor would request units from all of the new territories which had been given over to him so that they might march in some type of victory parade. My brother Philip thought I might be required to march in such a parade as the head of a north German unit," Friedrich said.

"Truly, Friedrich, did you really think that any of you would have to march in Paris?" Magdalene inquired of her husband.

"My dear, those were strange times. Napoleon believed he could reconstruct the empire of Charlemagne. I thought anything was possible. You remember I related to you that the Prince told us we must expect the worst. We were paying tribute to the French for our share of what were called 'improvements' in the Empire. At first I refused to pay but His Majesty took me aside to make clear that he needed my support. He said that too many of the lesser nobles were weak and needed the unequivocal support of some of the heads of the older families if we were to have any shred of independence," Friedrich said.

"Yes, it was too dreadful to contemplate," Magdalene said.

"Rudolph, you have been very attentive. Do you want to hear more?" Friedrich said.

"Yes, Papa, I do. But you said earlier there were some good things to say about Napoleon but so far all of what you have been telling me doesn't sound very good," Rudolph said. He was beginning to fidget somewhat with the long history lesson.

"Mostly I still harbor bad thoughts about Napoleon, but there was a flowering of education throughout all of what was being called the Empire, especially in science and literature. Napoleon helped with all of that. Several of the old universities were given a great boost. Places like Heidelberg, Mainz, Cologne, and Halle were rejuvenated. In Prussia, when William von Humbolt was made minister of education there was a great surge of new development in all of the sciences, especially chemistry and physics. Soon the dependency on the religious groups, both Protestant and Catholic, gave way and many new faculty members, especially scientists and philosophers, were added.

"Napoleon was also very interested in art. To be sure, he stole huge amounts of classic art from Rome, Egypt, and Amsterdam and placed them all in the Louvre Museum in Paris. It soon became the thing to do, and many wealthy patrons were attracted to accumulating their own fine collections. Music was greatly favored among the German states. Everywhere new opera houses and concert halls were being constructed. Napoleon was very clever. He would allow some of the states to use their tribute money for the construction of these fine buildings," Frederick added.

"It's hard to think that so much good could happen as the result of Napoleon being in power," Rudolph said.

"Yes, but look what happened when Alexander brought back new ideas from Persia and how Rome exported their ways and ideas throughout Europe during the time of the Caesars," Friedrich added.

"And the gardens. Don't forget the gardens, those beautiful French gardens," Magdalene added. "One comes again to the down side. I remember how you and Philip brought up the subject of why so many young people were emigrating to America."

"Many of our fine young people were leaving to escape being conscripted into Napoleon's army," Friedrich said.

"The American government was giving away huge tracts of land, if people would settle, hoping to entice many immigrants from Europe," Magdalene said. "We were concerned about your brothers, Heinrich and Clemens."

"Yes, I worried about them very much since they could have been conscripted. We began thinking we should send them to school in England, where they might avoid that possibility. Both Clemens and Heinrich were vulnerable, being 16 and 15," Friedrich said.

"What do you mean, they were vulnerable?" Rudolph asked.

"They were about as old as you are now and that was when most of the countries in western Europe were conscripting young men into the army, sometimes even as young as 13. We knew that was true in Prussia, Austria, and France," Friedrich said.

"Late in 1806 I decided that your brothers should go to England. Since their mother, Wilhemine, my first wife, was a Princess and was a cousin of His Highness, we both had to agree, before the Prince would hear of our marriage, that any children we might have could not claim any lineage to the throne. The boys had decided to use their mother's name."

"That change in their status made the move to having them go to school in England easier. Your mother's father, your grandfather, was very well connected with the English, so the whole arrangement was accomplished within a month and without any great difficulty. To be sure their departure left a considerable hole in this household, and you were greatly upset by all of this," Friedrich said.

"I'm not sure I've answered your questions very well, Rudolph. Even today people in Europe are divided by what they think of Napoleon," Friedrich said.

"Yes, I find it still somewhat confusing. What you call good hardly seems to compensate for all of the lives that were lost during those many years of war. Even so, I'd like to hear more about those days. You make it much clearer than Professor Wannamacher," Rudolph said.

"Well, Rudolph, we lived through those days and we were deeply affected by the events of the day. Perhaps in a day or so we can talk further," Friedrich said.

To make up for the loss of attention which his older brothers had shown him, both his mother and father, but his mother especially, showered attention upon him almost constantly. Fearing for his safety in those uncertain times, Magdalene persuaded her husband that Rudolph should be tutored at home rather than attend the local Academy where he had been. When Rudolph was 13, he was sent back to the Academy.

Beethoven Plays at the Palace

A few days later Rudolph again found his parents receptive to talking more about the Napoleonic years.

"Papa, were there some other things you can remember about what was going on in the country before the Battle of Waterloo?" Rudolph asked one night towards the end of dinner.

"We're just ready for coffee. Let's have it served in the drawing room. I'll ask Ernst to bring the coffee items to the drawing room, if you like," Magdalene said.

"Excellent idea," Friedrich said as he pushed back his chair and left the dining room for the drawing room. All the others followed.

Everyone clustered about the stove, sitting in a small circle.

"Magdalene, do you remember the time we heard Beethoven play the pianoforte at the palace?" Friedrich asked.

"Yes, of course I do. It was a peculiar and yet a memorable evening," Magdalene said.

"Let's go back to the midsummer of 1807. Napoleon had decided to have a meeting with Czar Alexander at Tilsit, which, as you know, is some sixty miles south and east of Koenigsberg. Although the two armies were ready for action, none was required as the two emperors decided to make common cause. Napoleon agreed that the Russian possessions should remain as they were, and in return he received the support of Czar Alexander in maintaining the peace in Europe.

"However, Napoleon was less generous with Frederick Wilhelm of Prussia, whom he regarded as a traitor after he had sided with the English. He was compelled to surrender to the French all of the Prussian territory west of the Elbe. Most of Prussian Poland was ceded to the Grand Duchy of Warsaw, which in turn became a French protectorate.

"Yes, we had concluded that with the French controlling almost all of Europe, we had made the right decision to have Clemens and Heinrich go to school in England," Friedrich said.

"And, my dear, I recall how hard it was for you to allow the boys to go. We had great uncertainty about when we would see them again," Magdalene said. "We hoped they would come home over Christmas, though, of course, that did not happen. Political conditions were too unsettled."

"It was about that time when I received an invitation from the Prince," Friedrich said.

"What did it say?" Rudolph asked. He was now sitting on the edge of his seat.

"It was very formal. I recall that we were invited to a concert late in August. Herr Beethoven from Bonn was to be the featured artist. We thought it was a little unusual for His Highness to be doing that. Remember?" Magdalene said.

"Indeed, it was most unusual. There had not been a concert or a party of any sort at the Palace for at least a year. The last time we'd been invited was for the Christmas celebration a year earlier, and then only a small quartet was playing off to one side. You couldn't help but wonder what this was all about, especially since times were very bad. Money was scarce." Friedrich said.

"How old was I then?" Rudolph asked.

"Let me think. I suppose you were about two years old, my dear, and just at the age of getting into things," Magdalene said.

"When the August date came around, it turned out to be a lovely day, neither too hot nor too cool. I busied myself with all manner of things in order to ready for the evening," Magdalene said.

****

Sitting in her room that day, following breakfast and with Stephanie in attendance, she asked, "Stephanie, do get out the light blue linen dress and the green silk, and we'll see which mood I'm in for tonight."

Immediately Stephanie returned with the two dresses, holding both high, one in each arm. "Begging your pardon, Ma'am, but the blue is ever so much prettier for this time of year," she said.

"Yes, I think you're right. Now what jewels should I wear? One can never be more elaborate than the Princess," Magdalene said, more to herself than to Stephanie. "Probably the pearls will do as well as anything. The diamonds would

look too ostentatious. Yes, I think the pearls will do quite
well."

"The pearls are very becoming," Stephanie added, and
went to fetch the jewel case.   She placed the case before
Magdalene who, taking a small key from around her neck,
opened the case and removed the pearls.

After a light supper, Magdalene and Friedrich were
ready to go to the palace. Magdalene made a grand entrance
down the staircase of her house, to the applause of her
husband. "You will be the most lovely of all of the women
this night." Friedrich said, raising both arms. As he did so,
Magdalene gave him a small curtsy and then, linked her arm
with his. Rudolph watched from the side as Nurse Hannah
held him by the hand. Magdalene went over to Rudolph,
picked him up and after giving him a long hug and kiss, walked
out with her husband to the waiting coach.

The invitation had stated that the concert would begin
at 7:30 P.M. but everyone knew that it would be at least 8
before anything would actually get under way. Arriving almost
exactly at 7:30, Friedrich was astonished to see so many
carriages already in the outer courtyard of the palace.

"How unusual to see so many of the courtiers here so
early. Perhaps Herr Beethoven is bringing us some word from
the Emperor. I understand he is, or at least he was, a great
admirer of the Emperor," Friedrich said to Magdalene as they
drew up to the outer gate.

They could see that there were at least six or seven
coaches which had pulled to one side of the inner court yard,
having discharged their passengers. The grooms were gathered
together, each in the colors and style of his household.

As Friedrich and Magdalene approached the front
portico, one of the Prince's footmen opened the carriage door
and, taking Magdalene's hand, helped her alight, a gesture he
repeated for Friedrich.

Entering the foyer of the lower reception hall,
Magdelene checked her attire in the large mirror at the foot of
the steps leading up to the great hall, where various receptions
were held. The highly ornate hall, decorated in the baroque
style with much gilt everywhere, was ablaze, lit by a series of
gilt candelabras. Everywhere were hanging baskets of flowers,

which made a spectacular impression. A small group of people were already lined up, waiting to be received by the Prince and Princess, who stood in front of their richly carved and gilded thrones.

For the most part, the presentations were perfunctory, but old protocol dating back to the times of the Holy Roman Empire and Charlemagne required a certain procedure and formality. The court chamberlain announced each guest. Because Friedrich was so well known at court, no prompting was necessary. The chamberlain, Baron von Ettersdorf, called out, "Baron Friedrich von Damsgaard and Baroness von Damsgaard."

Friedrich advanced first and bowed to the Prince. "Your Highness, we are grateful to be included in these wonderful festivities," Friedrich said. Turning to Magdalene he added, "May I present the Baroness von Damsgaard."
Magdalene curtsied with eyes lowered   . "Your Highness was kind to include us this evening," Magdalene said. The process was repeated with the Princess, but to Magdalene she said, "My dear Magdalene, I am so anxious for you to meet Herr Beethoven. You know, he is quite remarkable. We're told that he was sensational in Vienna. Even Herr Goethe sings his praise. But first you must meet Le Comte de Lyon, a special emissary from Paris."

There were more introductions, and one of the butlers came by to make certain that champagne was available for everyone. Very shortly the Chamberlain announced the beginning of the concert, and chairs were brought in for the 50 or 60 guests in attendance. When everyone had taken their seats, the Chamberlain said in a loud voice, "Meine Damen und Herren, tonight we have the privilege of having Herr Ludwig van Beethoven, who has recently returned from his triumphs at the courts in Vienna. He will inaugurate the new Beckstein pianoforte purchased by His Majesty for the occasion. Herr Beethoven will begin by playing his Concerto in G."

Herr Beethoven entered through a side door and walked the distance from the far end of the room to the front, making a few deferential bows to the assembled dignitaries of the court. He was dressed in formal clothes, but Magdalene remarked later that she thought he had slept in them. Most striking was his tousled hair, giving him the appearance of someone who did not want to be where he was. He walked straight towards the gilded piano and, bowing only slightly to the Prince, sat down, pulled up his sleeves and began his concerto with great gusto.

Few people in the room had ever heard this piece before as it had been composed only two years earlier and was seldom presented. Later he played the Sonata in F minor, which was received more enthusiastically.

When he finished, he once more bowed to the Prince and the Princess but then walked resolutely past all of the guests, disappearing as suddenly as he had appeared. On most occasions of this sort an artist would stop to chat with some of the guests, many of whom had rather extensive knowledge about music, and some were even accomplished musicians. The Prince was applauding vigorously but appeared somewhat startled by Herr Beethoven's quick disappearance.

Speaking to the Chamberlain, he said, "Do see if you can locate Herr Beethoven. I should like to have a chance to talk to him further, and I am sure Le Comte de Lyon would as well." He then motioned to the butlers to begin seating the guests who by now were talking among themselves.

Magdalene said to Friedrich, "My, that was quite an unforgettable performance! What I wouldn't give to be able to play the pianoforte with even half as much skill!."

"To be sure. To be sure," Friedrich muttered in reply. "Please come with me while I talk to Le Comte de Lyon." The two of them made their way across the room.

Bowing to Le Comte, Friedrich quickly introduced himself and in turn introduced Magdalene to him.

"A most impressive rendition this evening, would you not agree?" Friedrich said.

"Yes, yes, very impressive," Le Comte de Lyon replied as he glanced around, using his lorgnette to scrutinize them. He was dressed in a heavy green brocaded coat, a gold waistcoat, and black velvet knee pants.

"I understand that Herr Beethoven has been very impressed with the Emperor. Is it not true that he dedicated one of his symphonies to him?" Friedrich inquired.

"That is not entirely the case. I believe Herr Beethoven retracted his dedication, shortly after the Emperor had been proclaimed as Emperor. It is often very hard to understand the German mind!" Le Comte de Lyon said.

"Really? Do you think so? Perhaps if you were to spend more time among us, you might find that our inquisitive spirit is the one which predominates. It strikes me that what Herr Beethoven is trying to express in his music is very much of an inquisitive nature. But tell me, how do things look? Any problems with the English?" Friedrich said.

"Now that the Prussians have agreed to close their ports to English trade, I would think there will be little difficulty," Le Comte de Lyon said. "And since the Emperor has graciously returned Hannover to Prussian control, I think the Prussian King will be pleased to continue his close collaboration with the French, do you not agree, Herr Baron?"

"Yes, yes, of course! I am pleased to hear that, since some of the people here have family members in England and, naturally, they become concerned," Friedrich said.

"Of course. Now if you will excuse me," Le Comte de Lyon said and bowing briefly, wandered off to talk to some of the other guests.

"Obviously that was all of the time I was to get," Friedrich said to Magdalene. "I say, I'm as hungry as a bear. I do hope that dinner will be announced soon."

Almost on cue one of the butlers announced dinner. Friedrich linked arms with his wife, and they began the slow procession to the dining room, just a few hundred feet away. Invariably the procession would be slow as people talked to one another along the way. Upon entering the dining room they were informed where they were to sit. Herr Beethoven was to sit to the right of Princess Juliane, and Le Comte de Lyon to the right of the Prince at the opposite end of the table.

Magdalene was seated between her brother-in-law, Baron Philip von Damsgaard, and Graf von Bittermeier, who had come from Cologne to participate in the discussion with Le Comte de Lyon. Friedrich was seated between Baroness von Mitteldorf and Baroness von Schlegel, both of whom he thought were rather tiresome old ladies, although they were of the old school and from fine families of the area.

"My Lord," Magdalene said to Graf von Bittermeier, "What is the importance of having Le Comte de Lyon present tonight?"

"Very shortly we shall all learn, my dear Baroness," Graf von Bittermeier stated. "Look to the head of the table."

Just then the Prince stood up and, of course, all of the men stood up with him. He glanced around the room, raised his glass and immediately the room became silent.

"Ladies and Gentlemen of the Court of Ostend-Aachen, I give you the personal envoy of His Highness, The Emperor of France. We welcome his ambassador, Le Comte de Lyon on this auspicious occasion," he said.

Sitting down, he lifted a glass to Le Comte, a gesture which was followed by all of the guests.

Le Comte rose with great ceremony and with a sense of his own importance. Looking slowly about the room, he began his speech, "His Imperial Majesty, Emperor Napoleon, is always pleased to foster opportunities to increase the interchange of cultural events such as we have witnessed this evening with the concert by Herr Beethoven. We are all inspired by his wonderful music. His Majesty is grateful for the closer ties which bind our peoples together. We salute His Highness, Prince Franz, and all of you most noble and worshipful people from the Court of Ostend-Aachen." With great flourish he lifted a glass in the direction of the Prince and then extended his arm in a wide wave to all of those who were seated. He then saluted the Prince again with a wave of his other hand and sat down.

"What does all that mean?" Magdalene inquired of Philip.

"What it means is that the Prince has agreed to pay a sizable tithe to Paris twice a year, and that then means that your husband and all the rest of us will have to pay a certain tribute to the Prince for our part. At least we have not been invaded," Philip added, sotto voce, "Because Friedrich has just been advanced to Exchequer, he will have to pay more than I."

"Oh, my, that's certainly not very good news. I suppose it's not known how much that will be," Magdalene asked.

"No, I shouldn't think so. The Privy Council has not met and probably will not meet until the week after next, long after Le Comte has returned to Paris," Philip said.

"What a wretched business! When we were invited, Friedrich had little idea of what it was all about. I suppose Herr Beethoven was invited to play in order to show the French that there were some talented Germans around," Magdalene said.

"To some extent I'm sure that is true," Philip replied. "But there's another twist to it. You see Beethoven dedicated one of his symphonies to the Emperor but then changed the dedication to say 'to the memory of a great man'--which is quite a difference. Everyone says that Napoleon was infuriated. So you could say that Beethoven's being here may not be so complimentary after all!"

"Yes, I see. How interesting! I wonder how this is being interpreted in Paris," Magdalene said.

"Depending on how it's interpreted may indicate how much of a tribute we'll be forced to pay," Philip said.

"One wonders how much more bowing and scraping we are going to have to go through now that the Emperor is riding all over Europe and adding every little hamlet to his empire," Magdalene said.

"Yes, yes! One indeed wonders. One wonders who is listening to conversations. I don't trust Le Comte one little bit. Who knows what he takes back to Paris!" Philip said. He became visibly more agitated, and his face reddened as he was talking. "It's no wonder so many of the peasants are leaving for America!"

"I suppose so, but I can't imagine what would induce Friedrich or me to want to go anywhere. Could you or Rosalinde ever do such a thing?" Magdalene said.

"No, of course not! But our situation, yours and ours, is quite different from most of the people who work the lands for us," Philip said.

"Thank heaven for that!" Magdalene said.

The evening continued with light-hearted conversation among the guests. Several toasts were made, many of them to the Prince and Princess. Dinner was followed by some dancing in the long hall and before long it was 1 A.M. in the morning and the court began to disperse.

Friedrich and Magdalene had several dances together as well as with other partners. After one dance Friedrich said,

"The hour has become quite late, and it is time for us to be leaving. First we must make our way over to the Prince and his guest, Le Comte de Lyon." They walked slowly over to where the Prince and Le Comte were standing.

"Your Highness, we have enjoyed this evening immensely," Friedrich said, bowing to the Prince. To Le Comte de Lyon he said, "The Baroness and I are most grateful for this opportunity to be with you. We hope that his Imperial Majesty may have the opportunity to be with us at some time in the future."

Le Comte de Lyon said, "His Majesty will be grateful to learn of your felicitations."

Once in their carriage Friedrich was less flattering. "What a toad that pompous Comte turns out to be! These are fearsome times, Magdalene, fearsome."

"While at dinner I asked Philip if he could imagine any situation which would make him want to emigrate, to America, for example, if things were to become very bad here. As I expected, he said that he could not imagine any set of circumstances which would impel him to leave. What about us, Friedrich?" Magdalene inquired.

"Our situation is very secure, Magdalene. No, I cannot imagine anything that would be so bad as to make life here no longer bearable. Of course, what will stop Napoleon from his rampage is something none of us knows. But consider the Thirty Years War. Though there was a great amount of fighting, we, that is our ancestors, survived, and I suspect we will survive the Corsican just as some of my relatives survived the Swedes and the Saxons when they swooped into the land." Friedrich said.

"To be sure, my dear, I think our future looks assured," Friedrich said and gave his wife a tender kiss to help assuage her previous concern.

"I'm only slightly worried. I suppose being a new mother makes one feel a bit differently. You can't help but wonder what will happen to your child. Incidentally, Friedrich, I believe I'm pregnant again," Magdalene said.

"You really believe you're pregnant? This is by far the best news I have heard all night!" Friedrich said.

"I'm always happy to brighten your day," Magdalene said.

"To be sure, my dear, I think our future looks assured," Friedrich said and gave his wife a tender kiss to help assuage her previous concern.

****

"I love hearing about some of those days. Imagine hearing Beethoven in person!" Rudolph said.

"There are a good many other stories. Just now, however, it's time for bed," Friedrich said.

CHAPTER 3

The War of 1812 and Beyond

Often at the end of the day Friedrich and Magdalene would discuss the events of the day. It was a pleasant time to which they both looked forward. On this particular day Friedrich seemed more agitated than was usual. Magdalene found him pacing back and forth in his study.

"Friedrich, you seem preoccupied tonight," Magdalene said.

"Well, yes I am. Now that both Great Britain and France have blockaded our ports, almost all of the other European countries, including us, have suffered economic hardships." Friedrich said.

"What does that mean in every day terms?" said Magdalene.

"To begin with it means that the value of our currency and that of most of the countries of Europe is 10 to 15 % less than at the beginning of the year. We have to pay more for everything. But, in addition, Napoleon is strengthening the garrison in Danzig, and now we hear that new military units were dispatched from the Elbe to the Oder," Friedrich said.

Later at dinner Magdalene said, "One cannot help but worry as to what will happen next." There was little animation at dinner on this night.

As events continued to unfold, the Russians refused to continue the pursuit of the continental blockade. Napoleon was furious, and this factor catapulted the French and the Russians into the War of 1812.

Coming home from the Palace late on a very cold evening in February 1812, Friedrich went directly to his study and, disconsolate, sat looking out of the window. Just then Magdalene came in and sat down beside him. "Friedrich, you look terrible. What bad news has come your way today?" she said, taking his hand in hers.

"You cannot imagine what the Prince told us today," Friedrich said. Rising from his chair, he began to pace around the room. "All of the German states have been ordered to send conscripts to join the Emperor's forces. We were informed that there are to be about 300,000 men!"

"Three hundred thousand!" Magdalene repeated. "But

what does this mean?" Now she, too, became agitated and started to fan herself even though the room was quite cold.

"Everyone feels certain that the Emperor is planning to invade Russia some time this year. The Prince has put out the order for all young men 16 to 24 to join the Army. Many are fleeing to the forests, trying to escape. Some of the older veterans are still tied up in Spain so that this new campaign will be fought by these young recruits. It will be a slaughter!" Friedrich said.

"And why is it that Russia must be invaded?" Magdalene asked.

"They say that the Emperor is calling it a holy war to preserve Western Civilization from the great wave of Slavic barbarism. Can you think that anyone believes such nonsense?" Friedrich said.

"What a truly dreadful affair! Tell me, Friedrich, do you think the older boys are still safe in England? Is there any way this monster can reach out and conscript them?" Magdalene asked.

"I think they are quite safe. I'm sure Napoleon thinks he will invade Britain after he conquers Russia. But it is too monstrous to contemplate. We are told that some of his advisers in Paris are warning of ruin if he proceeds, but I have little doubt that he will l go ahead. He has such colossal ambition. Some say that an army of almost 700,000 men will be assembled to invade as soon as the spring rains subside. How will the land accommodate that horde of men and animals. Think how much this campaign will cost him! And for what?"

Wiping his brow with a lace kerchief, he continued. "As though that is not bad enough, the Prince must send more gold to Paris to help finance this awful affair. All of the nobles in this region will have to come up with our share. I don't know where we are expected to find the money."

"My dear, we must do the best we can. Now no more of my ranting for now. Let's go to dinner. I know you have seen to its preparation."

"Yes, of course, do come with me." They linked arms and walked slowly towards the dining room which had been ready for well over an hour. "But, Friedrich, if we are taxed any further, where will it stop?" The dinner was roast pork, apples and dumplings, which were Magdalene's favorites.

Late in June Friedrich returned home from the Palace again with bad news he discussed at dinner. "Napoleon's armies were at the Vistula in May, and now they have crossed the Nieman into Russia. What utter folly!"

"What kind of mania comes over a man like that?" Magdalene asked.

"Yes, he may be the ruin of all of Europe before he's done!" Friedrich said.

"Papa, will you have to go to war?" Rudolph asked.

Placing his arm around Rudolph's shoulders, Friedrich said, "No, my son. Neither you nor I will go to war. That's why Heinrich and Clemens are in England - to avoid the outreach of the French war machine."

There were several battles along the way to Moscow. The attempt to reduce the Czar's hold on his people and his lands was not successful despite what was regarded as a carnage of the worst sort. Great destruction of Moscow was not enough to bring victory to Napoleon as the days of fall became cold and bitter. Late in October Napoleon decided that to remove his now small army before the winter snows would decimate them completely. The retreat from Moscow was one disaster after another. Napoleon reached Paris on December 18th in a state of dejection.

Czar Alexander lost no time in making the most of his opportunity, which led him to conspire with the Prussians and the Poles to make common cause against Napoleon. As King of Prussia, Frederick Wilhelm III did what he could to align himself with what appeared to be the winning side. Gradually large forces, including those of Austria, came together against Napoleon, and in October 1813 Wellington, fresh from victories in Spain, moved into France. Further battles brought the allied group of Russia, Prussia, Sweden, and Austria to Paris.

At dinner that night Magdalene and the children, now consisting of Rudolph and his young brother and sister, Eduard and Bertha, were given the news which Friedrich was eager to tell them.

"Only today the Prince has announced that Napoleon

has abdicated! We have learned that the fierce battle at Leipzig was disastrous for Napoleon. My darlings, these bad times should be at an end." Friedrich said.

After hearing this startling news, Magdalene clapped her hands together and looking at her husband said, "Praise be to God."

"Does that mean the Clemens and Heinrich will be coming home again?" Rudolph said, looking hopefully at his father.

"I wish I could say, yes, for sure, Rudolph, but we have yet to understand how secure we really are. Wars are very disturbing, and sometimes the peace is uncertain as well," Friedrich said.

Napoleon was exiled to Elba, where, for nine months, a peace of sorts settled on all of Europe. The peace was short lived. Napoleon escaped from Elba and landed in Provence.

As Napoleon marched towards Paris, he gathered forces along the way. By March 1815 he had returned to Paris to claim the Tuileries as his palace. The 100 days of Napoleon's return to France ended in June 1815 at Waterloo where he was soundly defeated by a combined force again led by Wellington and supported by von Bulow.

Late one afternoon in August Friedrich came home and at dinner announced, "Napoleon has been taken to St. Helena off the coast of Africa by the English, and now he will remain in some sort of captivity for the rest of his days."

"But can we believe it this time?" Magdalene replied. Increasingly she thought of her two sons, Rudolph and Eduard, ten and six, as well as her stepsons, now 24 and 25, still living in England. "If only it is true. We've suffered greatly these several years with all of these armies going back and forth, destroying the land. And then nothing but more taxes."

"In these hard times it's hard to be jubilant when the uncertainties have been so great for so long. Nonetheless, we must hope. Perhaps Clemens and Heinrich may yet come back to Germany," Friedrich said.

A few weeks later, a letter was received from Clemens. In his study Friedrich read to Magdalene, "My dear Father and Mother,

"Wonderful news! I shall be coming to Ostend-Aachen

soon. You should now know that I joined the forces in England to fight against the French. For almost two years I have been in the Royal Fusiliers . In fact, at the Battle of Waterloo, the Duke of Wellington presented me with a medal for bravery. I look forward very much to seeing you once again. Please give my love to all of my brothers and sister. Your devoted son, Clemens Anton."

In September 1815, Clemens returned to his father's house once more. By now he had grown to be a handsome young man, made even more so in the elegant scarlet uniform of the British Army. On his arrival Magdalene reached him first, embracing him with outstretched arms.

"Oh, my dear son, let me look at you again! To think that you are really alive and back with us!" Magdalene said, smothering him with kisses mixed with tears.

Hearing the exclamations of his wife and son from the library, Friedrich burst on the scene and embraced Clemens with tears welling up in his eyes. "Clemens, this is one of the happiest days for your mother and me! You are not a prodigal son, but we welcome your return with no less enthusiasm. What good fortune this is and what joy we all have this very moment," Friedrich said, kissing and hugging him simultaneously.

Magdalene made certain that as much of a banquet as possible was prepared. In former days the larder was always full, but the last ten years had taken their toll. All members of the aristocracy were severely pinched as one tax levy after another had come along, all of which had been imposed to finance the several Napoleonic wars. Some venison and chickens were located, and with the skill of Magdalene and the kitchen staff, it became a festive evening.

Before the dinner started and all were seated, Friedrich stood and lifted up his glass of wine. "The good Lord has seen fit to return our son to us for which we are very grateful. For him we wish the very best of prosperity and happiness. Clemens, we all salute you and welcome you back in our family," Friedrich said in a voice more high pitched than usual, indicating his considerable emotion at this declaration. Magdalene got up and went around to where Clemens was sitting and kissed him on both cheeks. As she was hugging him, she squeezed his arms and said, "Clemens. you have really grown up literally and figuratively. You are even more handsome than I remember you!" Clemens blushed with all of that maternal praise.

Clemens was attentive to everyone but especially to his half-brother Rudolph. Having grown up in a time of almost perpetual war, Rudolph was very interested in everything military and could not sort out who were the victors and who were the victims of Napoleon's rapacious appetite for war. The younger children, Bertha and Eduard, seemed more interested in some of their own games and conversation, but Rudolph was glued to every word from his brother.

After dinner all went into the drawing room for coffee. Almost immediately Rudolph asked, "What did you do during the battle of Waterloo?" Clemens took great delight in being the center of attention. Placing his arm around Rudolph as they walked into the drawing room, he said, "To begin with, Rudolph, the Duke of Wellington was an even more clever tactician than Napoleon. He had many victories in Spain and he knew that the battle had to be decisive."

Rudolph pulled his brother to the floor so that he could demonstrate the location of all of the various regiments at the Waterloo hill. Clemens took cushions and placed them around in various places to show where the allied forces were and where the French were located. He moved the cushions around in such a fashion in order to provide some idea of what had taken place on that day in August. "See, this is where the headquarters of the English were located, and I was with the Fusilier over here," Clemens said. He moved the cushions again and again to demonstrate the way the battle went.

With obvious admiration for his brother, Rudolph said, "I would like to be a soldier when I grow up, just like you." He seemed transfixed as Clemens relayed his story.

"Well, perhaps you can, Rudolph, but you will have to study hard about military matters," Clemens said. It was later than usual when the family broke up to go to bed. As they walked upstairs, Rudolph clung to Clemens all the way to his bedroom. As they parted, Clemens leaned over to give his younger brother a hearty hug and kiss.

Six weeks later word came from Heinrich that he, too,

would be returning home. Once he arrived, there was again much celebration. That Christmas church bells pealed longer than usual. There was great joy everywhere as everyone concluded that this was one of the happiest years ever.

CHAPTER 4

Recovery after Napoleon

While Friedrich, Clemens, and Heinrich were having breakfast one morning, Friedrich read aloud from the morning newspaper, " 'All reports suggest that conditions have improved in Europe now that the threat of Napoleon recedes ever more into the past.' Of course, there continues to be talk about the Bonapartists, and I hear that the new King, Louis Phillipe, who is from Orleans, has restored some of the emblems of the imperial regime."

"Yes, such as replacing the statue of Napoleon on the top of the Vendome Column," Heinrich said.

"And eventually, I'll warrant, Napoleon's remains will be returned to France," Clemens added.

"I shouldn't doubt that," Friedrich added. "But you know while Napoleon was conquering Europe, new ways of manufacturing have begun. Steam engines, especially in England, are changing the way everything is being manufactured. Now some people are calling this an Industrial Revolution which may eclipse any influence Napoleon's antics may have had as a truly significant force in Europe."

"You know, father, some people say that Napoleon would not have lost at Waterloo if the British had not been superior in their supply system, the quality of their weapons and other materiel of war," Clemens said.

"That may be so, but the fact that the British are now much more financially stable than any other country must be part of that as well," Friedrich added.

"I think that's a big feature," Heinrich said. "Both of us were impressed while we were in England with the wealth of that country. The country houses are grand beyond anything we have in Europe, except for the palaces of the princes and kings. When we were in school, I was astonished at the size of the libraries which were available to us."

Later that day in the evening when everyone had gathered together in the drawing room, a new line of conversation began. "Now here is an interesting question for all of you," Magdalene said. Rudolph immediately turned towards her as she spoke, wondering what he would hear next. "You two older boys were educated in England, but what shall we do for Rudolph? Should he, too, go to England? Possibly he might go to France, where new academies in science are said to be flourishing. Or should he stay right here? What are the advantages or disadvantages of each?"

"I missed being home very much and at times was quite homesick," Heinrich was quick to state. "Surely the Ostend-Aachen Academy is quite good, certainly for one's early years."

"It depends to a large extent on what Rudolph wants to do. He has talked about a military career, but is that what he really wants?" Clemens said. "If things had been different, I might not have selected a military career."

"I do think there are great advantages to remaining with the family. We had no choice with you older boys," Friedrich said.

"Well, it's something to think about. Maybe he will want to do something in the business world, where there seem to be great opportunities now. It is only a short time until manufacturing will spread in Europe and rival the English, I shouldn't wonder," Magdalene said.

"Yes, I suspect you're absolutely right," Friedrich said. "Though we don't see much evidence of any great potential in the German states except for the Ruhr and Rhine valleys. You have to have iron and coal and where else will you find it?"

"Now here is something to consider. What if Rudolph wanted to work with me at court? He could, you know. I'm sure the Prince would be able to accommodate someone like him just as his father did for some of us," Friedrich said.

"Certainly that's a possibility, but is that going to do much for the further development of manufacturing in Europe?" Magdalene said.

"Well, the court of Ostend-Aachen is a nerve center and new developments will always be discussed there, my dear," Friedrich said. "Let us at least think about it."

Rudolph rather enjoyed being the center of attention, but at the same time he did not express any inclination to any of the suggestions offered.

No decision was made on Rudolph's schooling or what his future career might be, but he did start in the Ostend-Aachen Academy the next fall. Magdalene was very happy to have her first-born son remain close to her. Rudolph's older brothers had various suggestions about what he should do, which they shared with Rudolph and their parents from time to time. Rudolph did well in his academic work, especially in the arts. When it came time to do studying, he often would be found drawing. Most of his drawings would be scenes from nature.

Rudolph was a good student and was always asking questions of his parents, his uncles and aunts, and especially his two older brothers. Heinrich said, "You know, Rudolph, if you are to work at the palace, you will need to know everything about our history."

"What do you mean by our history?" Rudolph asked.

"You remember when we came back from England and talked about the Waterloo battle? Well, that is one small piece of history. You have to know all about our family, the Prince's family, the German emperors starting from Karl der Grosse, the English kings and queens, and, of course, back to the Roman times!"

"That sounds like a lot of work," Rudolph said, looking rather forlorn as he said so. He quickly brightened and said, "Will you help me?"

"Of course I will," Heinrich said. "Now use your influence in the kitchen and see if you can get two pieces of cake so we can celebrate this matter."

Rudolph scampered off in the direction of the kitchen and in less than two minutes was back carrying two plates, each with two small tortes on them. "See what I've brought," Rudolph said, holding the plates proudly.

"You have more influence that I do," Heinrich said and quickly devoured his two tortes. "Now that we have had some fuel we should get to work. Come with me to the library and let's start with some geography." The two found the library unoccupied, and Heinrich went over to the large globe which stood on a pedestal near a window facing the garden. "How many of the countries in Europe can you name?"

"I think this is France over here. That's where Napoleon came from, didn't he?" Rudolph asked and pointed out France on the globe.

"Yes, that's right on both counts. Napoleon really

came from Corsica, which is down here in the Mediterranean, but we will always think of him as being from France. Now what countries are these?" Heinrich said. Rudolph's understanding of the countries of Europe was a bit hazy, but he did identify several correctly. "Now where is America?"

"America?" Rudolph asked.

Pointing to the North American continent, Heinrich said, "All of this is North America, and the middle part is the United States, but many people refer to this section as the United States of America, and you need to know more and more about it because so many people from Europe are immigrating to America."

"Will we emigrate to America?" Rudolph asked, not quite sure what such a question signified.

"I very much doubt it. But look, I think I will ask mother if I can set up a regular teaching program for you. Would you like that?" Heinrich asked. Rudolph nodded.

"Shall we find her now?" Heinrich asked.

"Oh, yes, let's do. I think she's still in her room," Rudolph said. He placed his hand into Heinrich's larger hand and the two bounded up the stairs to Magdalene's morning room and found her reading over some papers.

Knocking on the open door, Heinrich poked his head into the room and said, "Mother, are you ready to receive two of your sons?"

Somewhat startled, as few visitors were likely to be admitted to her morning room, Magdalene, wearing a light blue morning dress, quickly held out her hands to the two boys. "I am honored to have the two of you wishing to attend me. Please draw up chairs and tell me what is on your minds. I see you have obtained some tortes from the kitchen, judging from the crumbs on both of you," Magdalene said and reached over to Rudolph to brush off the crumbs from his jacket.

Heinrich began, "Mother, we really have a serious proposition to bring to you. Rudolph has asked me to help him with some of his studies, and I have already quizzed him on some simple geography and found his concepts of the countries of Europe to be somewhat hazy. I wondered, and he has suggested this himself, whether you and father would consent to my helping him in various studies on a regular basis.

I think we both would like that."

"Is that true?" Magdalene said, turning to Rudolph who, smiling broadly, looked like the very eager student, which, in fact, he was.

"Yes! Yes! I want to know all about history and Heinrich has been to England and says I must learn all about the English kings and queens and all the German emperors," Rudolph said, glancing towards Heinrich for confirmation.

"Well, Well!" Magdalene said. "I think this is a first-rate idea. Let's discuss this with your father at dinner tonight. What do you say?"

Early during dinner, Magdalene said, "Friedrich, Heinrich and Rudolph have spoken to me this morning about an interesting idea. Heinrich has offered to be something of a tutor to Rudolph to augment his basic knowledge of history, geography, and perhaps other subjects as well. I have said that we should discuss it tonight to see what you think," Magdalene said.

"On the surface of things, such an arrangement sounds very good. It might be useful for both of them. Rudolph could certainly benefit by having his work at the Academy reinforced. Heinrich might find that a teaching occupation would be much to his liking," Friedrich said. Looking around at everyone, he tried to see if their faces told him what his wife's words had conveyed. "I see you all nodding, so it's clear that this point has been well considered. Yes, yes, Magdalene, I think this idea of yours is a good one. Now we should work out exact times for the tutoring to help everyone with his respective obligations in the matter. I think I should pay Heinrich for some of his time, and I will work that out at another time. It would also be important for Rudolph to learn English from both Clemens and Heinrich. Since the older boys know English quite well now, we should make certain that we use their skills appropriately. As a matter of fact, Magdalene, it would be a good idea if you and I tried to learn a bit more English. I feel certain we'll be dealing with our English cousins even more in the future in such matters as commerce and manufacturing," Friedrich said.

"I'm delighted to hear that you think this is a good idea. I like everything you said except I'm not sure how much time you and I will have to learn English well, but we should try," Magdalene said.

"Thank you, sir. I'm ready to start as early as tomorrow morning," Heinrich said.

"And I too, sir," Rudolph echoed, his face fairly wreathed in smiles.

Rudolph turned out to be a good student and very much enjoyed the attention he received from his two older brothers. "Today we'll review the capitals of all of the countries of Europe," Heinrich said one wintry afternoon as they sat in the library. "We'll start at the top, England."

"London," Rudolph answered.

"Sweden."

"Stockholm."

So it went, with only one mistake among all of the countries. "Now I have just read 'The Isle of Greece' written by Byron and recently published in London. Listen to this,

'The mountains look on Marathon,
  And Marathon looks on the sea;
And musing there an hour alone,
  I dreamed that Greece might still be free,' " Heinrich read.

"Don't stop! What magnificent poetry," Rudolph said. Heinrich not only continued, but read other poems of Byron and also Wordsworth, Schiller, and Goethe. Whenever there was time, Heinrich read to his brother who was ever the receptive pupil, enjoying the words, the sentiments, and the verse. The two of them wept as Heinrich read from Schiller's "Die Jungfrau von Orleans." Reading and dreaming of great adventures became a part of Rudolph's being and life.

Young Men Make Plans

The fortunes of western Europe, including Ostend-Aachen, improved in the years following the Napoleonic era. The abundant stands of timber in the central and southern areas were an important resource for many of the German states. Most of the forested areas were owned by the aristocracy, and, whenever money was required, the owner would sell off the timber for construction purposes, allowing the cleared land to be used for agricultural purposes.

"Father, do you think the Prince will sell off the forest east of here?" Heinrich asked one evening at dinner.

"I rather think he will, why do you ask?' Friedrich replied.

"Some of the land originally belonging to Herzog Francis has now been cleared and is nothing but open land. I hear that it's not useful for any type of planting because of the nature of the soil," Heinrich said.

"True, but I think that's the exception. There are many tracts of land which are now used for vineyards, especially along the Moselle and the Rhine," Friedrich said.

"I have become interested in land management and forest preservation, and, from what I know, it seems to me that we should be much more concerned about the use of land. After all, there is only so much land in all of Europe. How will people live 50 to 100 years from now if they have no forests?" Heinrich asked.

"Your questions are worthy of the philosophers, Heinrich," Friedrich said. "Have you thought of pursuing some sort of studies which would allow you to make that a career?"

Blushing slightly, Heinrich said, "Sir, you read my mind. I've been seriously wondering about studies at Jena or Heidelberg. I have been reading some of Hegel, and, though I don't understand all of what he says, I am interested in learning more. Do you think that makes some sense?" Heinrich said.

"Yes, I do. Shall we continue this discussion over our coffee in the library?" said Friedrich. Turning to Magdalene, he added, "Would such a discussion be one you would care to join?"

"Of course. I will have the coffee brought to us."
Magdalene said. She pushed back her chair and rang for Ernst,
who came in from the kitchen and stood by her chair.

"Ernst, we'll have coffee in the library tonight,
Magdalene said.

The younger children took their cue from her and
scampered off to the library. Bertha and Eduard quickly seated
themselves close to the stove, always the warmest part of the
room. Clemens, Heinrich, and Rudolph grouped themselves
around the large table in the center of the room as Ernst and
Marie brought in the coffee dishes. Friedrich and Magdalene
seated themselves next to one another on the sofa.

Tonight it was Clemens' turn to distribute the coffee
cups along with the sugar and cream. Magdalene poured the
coffee. Rudolph passed the small tortes to everyone.

"Now then, Heinrich, tell us more what you think you
want to do with your life," Friedrich said.

"As I was saying, sir, I think I would like to study at
one of the German universities to advance my understanding of
philosophy, but including study of land use. While I have
thought of Jena and Heidelberg, I have no firm opinion,"
Heinrich said.

"Thuringia is quite some distance away," Magdalene
said. "I should not again like to have you too far away. It
would take several days to get there."

"Yes, Jena has a fine university, but the University at
Heidelberg is older and more established in many ways. Many
years ago I had a chance to spend a few days there. It certainly
has a beautiful location along the Neckar. Perhaps I can make
some inquiries at court about the most desirable places. Would
you like me to do that?" Friedrich said.

"Yes, of course, I would like that very much," Heinrich
said.

"Father, as you are going to make some inquiries at
court, perhaps you'd care to inquire about opportunities for a
military person such as myself," said Clemens.

"To be sure, but what do you have in mind?" Friedrich
asked.

"Well, it's January 1820 and I'm 30 years old and
trained in nothing but military matters," Clemens said.

"Yes, your career was molded by Napoleon and then polished by Wellington. I have already made some inquiries, but I'll pursue that matter closely, now that you bring it up," Friedrich said.

"If you go off to Heidelberg or some place like that what will I do for a tutor?" Rudolph said, directing his comment to Heinrich.

"I would have to arrange a special study plan for you if I go, and then I could check up on you by writing long letters to see what you've done," Heinrich said and reached over to squeeze his brother's shoulder.

"Friedrich, now that you are the Director of Finance for the Prince, I cannot imagine that there would be any problem in getting information on all of these points, would you?" Magdalene said, pouring another cup of coffee for him and for herself.

"No, I suppose not, but we'll have to see. The chamberlain always has good ideas, and I shall talk to him first," Friedrich said.

Late in March of the same year Friedrich announced at dinner that he had some important information for everyone. Grouped about the fire in the drawing room, everyone awaited his remarks.

The first one to speak was Eduard. "What do you have to say about me, Papa?"

"Come sit beside me, and you can hear the news, Eduard, though it has more to do with your older brothers. Clemens, there is an interesting prospect in South America which may be of interest to you. The Peruvian ambassador, Senior Martinez, has indicated that they are anxious to have experienced army officers from Europe, and especially from central Europe, to help reorganize and energize their Army. It seems that new mining is taking place in the Andes Mountains and many people are making claims on the land, with the result that they fear uprisings. I told Senior Martinez about your experiences, and he said you'd be exactly the sort of person they want. He would like to have a chance to talk to you anytime. How does that strike you, Clemens?" asked Friedrich.

"That sounds like my cup of tea! When would I be able

to talk to him?" Clemens said.

"I'll make immediate inquiries when I go to the palace tomorrow," Friedrich said. "Now, Heinrich, all my contacts from the Prince's counselors and the chamberlain seem to think that University in Heidelberg would answer your needs. If that sounds like what you want to do, inquiries would have to be made, but probably you could plan on being there this fall or earlier to find a place to live and become situated."

"Oh, my, I'm overwhelmed with all that news! It would be very hard to see our family shrink again, but I suppose we have to expect that. What do you say, Heinrich?" Magdalene asked.

"I'm a bit overwhelmed as well but also very excited. I have sometimes thought I was getting too old to think of University studies but think how old Luther was when he began some of his studies," Heinrich said.

On the following day Magdalene found time to be alone with Clemens. As they talked, she said, "You'll think I'm silly for bringing up this matter, but, my dear, if you are going to Peru, you will need to have a wife. I don't know much about Peru, but I would think having a wife would be essential to establish your family there. Does this sound very strange to you?"

"No, Mother, it doesn't sound strange. All last night as I lay in bed, I began to wonder what I would do in such a strange place. The army part I think I could manage, but being all alone in a new and strange land is something I wasn't looking forward to," Clemens said.

"Clemens, now you will think I'm an awful matchmaker, but what do you think about Baroness Katerina von Stehle? You know that your father and I have known her family for many years and we think highly of them," Magdalene said.

Blushing to his ears and looking distinctly embarrassed, Clemens asked, "Now you will think I am peculiar, but how does one get started in something of this sort?"

Reaching over to kiss him on the cheek, Magdalene said, "Leave that to me. First, we can start with a small dinner party for the family. But, of course, my dear, you will have to do your part once you have the opportunity."

Not long afterwards Magdalene wrote to Baron and Baroness von Stehle suggesting that the springtime would be a good time for them and their lovely daughter Katerina to come for dinner. Baroness von Stehle replied that they would be delighted, and so the seeds of romance were planted. At Christmas time of that year Clemens requested the hand of Katerina from her father, and the young couple announced their intent to marry in spring 1821. By then the Peruvian government, via their ambassador, had made an offer

Clemens to accept a commission as colonel and to be in charge of one of the regiments of the Peruvian Army. It was made clear by way of the ambassador that much reorganization and modernization of the regiment were needed.

In the meantime Heinrich made inquiries at the University in Heidelberg, and he was soon admitted as a student with advanced standing in the philosophy department. He was delighted. "I have only one regret, Rudolph," he said shortly after learning of his acceptance. "You have been such a wonderful student, and I should like to continue working with you. I'm not sure how to work it out, but I think we can write to each other so that I can learn how you are doing with your various studies. After I find a place to live in Heidelberg, I hope you will come to see me, and I can show you what university life is all about. Would you like that?"

"Would I like that? You don't have to ask twice! I'd like nothing better. I've never seen any university before so all of that sounds rather exciting to me. I'll really miss you as my special tutor, however," Rudolph said.

Although Rudolph took great interest in both of his older brothers and their fortunes, he was always much closer to Heinrich. At Easter 1821 a visit of the two brothers was arranged, and they had their first visit to the Grand Duchy of Baden and the famous university city of Heidelberg. It took almost a month to make all of the arrangements. New clothes had to be purchased which meant visits to the tailor, and travel possibilities had to be planned.

The house of Damsgaard was soon to be depleted by two of its members in 1821. On the third of May, after everything had been arranged, the two brothers would catch the morning post at the Inn in Minden. From there they would head for Osnebruck and eventually to the cathedral city of Cologne. In Cologne they were put up in a small inn close to the Rhine River and just a stone's throw from the cathedral.

The next morning during breakfast Heinrich and Rudolph were talking about what plans they should make. "We could spend the morning in Cologne and take the afternoon post. If we did that, we would have some time to visit the great cathedral. How does that sound, Rudolph?"

"I like exploring new places. All I know about Cologne is that it is now part of Prussia, at least I think that is what father said not long ago," Rudolph answered.

"Yes, I think that is correct. During some of the Napoleonic wars, the French occupied the city but then the Prussians took over following the battle of Waterloo. The city is really an old one extending back to Roman times. In fact, I read somewhere that around AD 50 Agrippina who was the wife of the Emperor Claudius, asked that the city become a Roman colony in honor of her. I believe she was born in the region. Later Cologne became part of the Hanseatic league and the city became prosperous.

"Let's finish breakfast and then go over to the cathedral to have a look," said Heinrich.

They walked across the square and stared up at the magnificent spires of the cathedral. "I believe this is the largest of the Gothic cathedrals in northern Europe. Let's go inside," said Heinrich.

Once inside Rudolph said, "I've never seen anything as magnificent as this cathedral, Heinrich. Look at those stained glass windows! They sparkle like jewels in the early light."

As they walked towards the high altar, they encountered a young priest who offered to show them about the cathedral. He said, "The first bishop came to Cologne in about 313 AD During the time of Charlemagne an archbishopric was established. Later in the Middle Ages the city governments had many fights with the church . It was always a question as to whose authority would be recognized. Eventually the city became a free imperial city. We hope those days are behind us."

Heinrich said, "Father, we are most grateful to learn so much about this wonderful cathedral. You have been most helpful. Many thanks!"

They then returned to the Inn and waited for the afternoon post. From Cologne they traveled along the Rhine to Mannheim, reaching Heidelberg on the eighth day.

CHAPTER 6

A Week in Heidelberg

Entering Heidelberg from the west, both Rudolph and Heinrich were immediately impressed with the beauty of the city along the Neckar. Several small boats were on the river, sailing westward and would likely head north up the Rhine. Others were docked, and barrels and boxes were being unloaded by muscular stevedores. When the post came to a stop at the Hotel Ritter just opposite the Heilig Geist Church, it was early in the afternoon. They noticed that several merchants and farmers were clustered around the church eager to sell their goods or produce to whomever might look in their direction.

Once their valises were lowered from the carriage, Heinrich began looking for someone who could take them to their pensione. Hailing a driver of a small cart, they were off, clattering down the cobblestone street to the Bell and Candle, a small pensione often frequented by incoming students. Once upstairs in their room, Heinrich immediately pulled off his boots and stretched out on one of the beds.

"Here we are, Rudolph. We may as well get a little rest before we go out for our first dinner in my new city," Heinrich said.

"You rest, Heinrich. I want to go downstairs and look around a bit. Maybe I can scout out a place for us to have dinner. I do have so many things I want to talk to you about. I'll come back about six o'clock," Rudolph said.

"Rudolph, you have too much energy! But get along. I'm almost asleep," Heinrich said.

Rudolph raced down the steps from their second floor room. Without waiting for any further directions, he wandered out into the street and at once had a sense of excitement as young men with their long scarves wrapped about their necks pushed by him on the street. He soon concluded that these must be students, and he wanted to be a part of what they were doing. One group stopped before a book store, and their conversation had something to do with the classes they were attending.

"Goethe, of course, is a great man, a great poet, but I find Schiller much more exciting. He's so much more of the times, don't you agree, Ramsgate?" one of the young men said.

"Perhaps. But you must become more than just acquainted with Goethe to appreciate the magnificence of his poems," Ramsgate said.

Rudolph had to restrain himself from entering into the conversation, as he considered that he was well read and could give an opinion on the matter if offered the opportunity. Although it was the middle of April, the weather had not warmed up so Rudolph kept walking, encountering one group of students after another. Periodically he would notice people whom he thought must be faculty members. They were decidedly more sedate in the demeanor, much more like his father, with their dark frock coats and trousers. Some were wearing beaver hats while others had caps. As he scurried up and down through the university area, he was more and more envious of his brother's being able to come to the university. He could not stop wondering whether one day he might have the same opportunity.

Having scouted the university area as well as other parts of the old city, Rudolph returned to the room and found Heinrich sound asleep on his bed. His first impulse was to shake his brother in order to wake him, but then thought that something a bit more diabolical would be fun. Spotting a small straw on the floor, he picked it up and began gently stroking his brother's ear with it as he sat on one edge of the bed. He didn't have to wait long before Heinrich began trying to brush the straw aside even though he was still half asleep. Becoming more impatient, Rudolph finally shook his brother's shoulder in order to rouse him from his slumber.

"What a pest you are, Rudolph," Heinrich said as he sat up and stretched, all the time keeping a wary eye on his brother lest he might try additional techniques for rousing him.

"And what a sleepy head you are. You'd think that you would have some greater interest in your new life in Heidelberg than to waste it in sleeping! This place is fairly alive with activity. Do you want to see for yourself or shall I give you a few highlights?" Rudolph said.

"Spare me the guide book approach. I'll come out and see for myself though I'm sure you'll tell me exactly what I'm seeing," Heinrich said.

After pulling on his boots and stretching, Heinrich

linked his arm with Rudolph's and together they raced down the stairs. Leaving the pensione, they were greeted with the still bright sunshine. Rudolph retraced his steps and everywhere pointed out different things which had interested him during his earlier investigations of the city.

"Now over here is where I found some students talking about Goethe and Schiller. Imagine! In no time you'll be coming home to tell us all about what you think of these two poets and probably others as well. How I envy you just now," Rudolph said.

"Yes, Rudolph, but it won't be long before you will be coming here or somewhere to be a student as well. You'll see. You're really more the studious type than I, you know," Heinrich said.

"I hope so, but I wish that were tomorrow. What fun it'd be to be here with you!" Rudolph said, and, running a few steps towards the bridge over the Neckar, he adroitly jumped up on the stone abutment, striking a mock heroic pose as his brother sauntered over to the bridge.

"Rudolph, you are an incurable romantic. Come down from there before you tumble into the water," Heinrich said and began to laugh as he offered his brother a hand.

"What's wrong with being a romantic, as you say?" Rudolph said.

"Nothing really. It's just that romantics are so impractical. They so often never get anything accomplished. Now Napoleon was certainly not a romantic!" Heinrich said.

"True. But look what happened to your unromantic Emperor!" Rudolph said.

"Perhaps he became a little too practical. But seriously, I think some of his deeds will live on for many years to come. Remember he was overcome by the English strategist, the Duke of Marlborough, who simply was even more practical. By the way, I think I am becoming hungry. Did you see any restaurants or kellers as you were walking about this afternoon?" Heinrich said.

"Well, yes, I did. I think there is a decent keller where we can get something to eat, just facing the Kornmarkt, not more than two steps from here," Rudolph said.

The brothers walked quickly to the keller, known as the

Sternlicht, which was a favorite among the student group in Heidelberg. It was a somewhat dimly lit place with many small tables which were quickly being filled. They ordered some bratwurst and sauerkraut and then some wine from a local vineyard.

"Heinrich, I know you will have a wonderful time here. Just look at how animated all of the young men whom we see here are. I can just imagine that you will be joining in with them soon. Where do you think your university career will lead you?" Rudolph asked.

"I do often think about that, but for the present I think I will see how all of this vast array of knowledge can be understood. As you know, I love books and studying, so I just want to absorb as much as I can at first and then I probably will settle on some subject for an advanced degree," Heinrich said.

Time passed quickly and soon it was necessary for Rudolph to think about his return to Ostend-Aachen. He had stayed long enough to see Heinrich enrolled in classes. Heinrich seemed to be interested in the history of ancient Rome.

"Heinrich, learning more about ancient Rome seems like a very impractical thing for you to do," Rudolph said on one of their last days together.

"A times I wonder about that myself. But think of what a wonderful civilization they had. Outstanding architecture! An empire extending almost over all of western Europe and around the Mediterranean. Their language has influenced almost all of the world and is still used in all of the Catholic churches. There is a practical aspect to be considered as well. How was it all accomplished is what I want to understand," Heinrich said.

"I see. I think I understand your point of view a little better. For me though, I think I must do something which may seem even more impractical to you. I do like all things about biology, of nature, especially the forests. You know it's astounding when one thinks that almost all of Europe was once covered with dense forests, but that's not true any more," Rudolph said.

"Good for you, Rudolph. Perhaps you will work in the Prince's forestry service one of these days, just like father.

Would you like that? And one of these days you may well find a charming lady to marry and to settle down to raising a family," Heinrich said.

"I think that's rather too far ahead of where I am. Right now I don't want to work at all. On my last night here, let's return to that little keller where all the students were," Rudolph said.

The keller was a short distance from where the two young men were staying. As they opened the door, they were greeted with a rush of cigar and pipe smoke and a cacophony of sound. On a day when many of the students had finished their examinations, the Sternlicht was always crowded, and the din of singing and merrymaking was common. By now the two brothers had learned much more about the city of Heidelberg and its university. As this would be Rudolph's last night, the two of them were anxious to have it be a memorable one. Even though they knew practically no one, they entered into the frivolity with singing, shouting, and drinking beer.

On the next morning Rudolph and Heinrich made their way back to the Hotel Ritter, which was where the post traveling northward would stop. Around eight P.M. when they arrived at the Ritter, it was barely light. Overnight a mist had settled over the city causing it to be damp and cold. The mist was thick enough so that it was difficult to make out more than the outlines of the church across the square. Neither of them spoke more than a few words. In about 30 minutes they could hear the clatter of the horses coming down the street. Soon the post came to stop before the hotel.

"Heinrich, I'm going to miss you very much," Rudolph said.

"And I will miss you as well. Promise me you'll write at least once a week," Heinrich said, giving his brother a big hug.

"Of course I'll write, but you must promise to write as well," Rudolph said.

Fresh horses were being brought out as the coachman placed Rudolph's small valise on top of the coach. Just before it was his turn to get into the coach, the young men once again hugged each other, both thinking that their lives were going to take different courses. They waved to each other one more time as the coach door was closed.

During the return trip Rudolph sat back in the coach and mused about what it would be like to be a real student in a university getting prepared for one's life as an adult. He could see himself in various situations, as a farmer, as a seaman, as a trusted aide at the court, as a poet, and many other possibilities as well.

When he finally arrived home, he burst into the house, eager to relate his adventures. He was first met by Eduard who fairly jumped into his arms beseeching him to tell about everything related to the trip.

"Eddie, how great to see you again. Let's find the others, and I can talk to you all at once," Rudolph said. For over an hour Rudolph was the center of attention as he tried to recreate the excitement which he had savored and at the same time to make sense to the others who had not had the good fortune to have been present.

"Oh, mother, I do so hope that one day I may be a student at Heidelberg or some other university!" Rudolph said.

"And so you shall, my dear, but not for a year or two. Remember you are only 16. Now there are some other things to think about. You may have forgotten that the Prince and Princess will be having their Spring Ball in just two weeks. I understand that some of the prettiest young ladies will be there," Magdalene said.

A Night to Remember

Soon after his return Magdalene invited Rudolph to have morning coffee with her in her morning room. She was most concerned with helping her son understand some special opportunities and obligations of a young nobleman of 16. The two of them were seated at a small table set before the windows facing the garden.

"The Prince's Spring Ball was once the most fashionable event of the springtime, as I have mentioned to you many times. It is meant for young lords and ladies, like you. During all of those dreadful years when Napoleon held sway over practically all of the continent, hard times prevented such festivities. This is the first year since the Battle of Waterloo that the Prince has felt confident enough to return to the traditions of the Spring Ball," Magdalene said.

"Well, naturally I'm happy that times are better, but what must I do and what would I expect?" Rudolph said, taking new interest in his mother's comments.

"To begin with, it will be an opportunity for you to get to meet several of the most delightful and charming young women from the land. And I might add the young ladies get to meet the most charming, handsome and eligible young men, and you will be one of them. It's not like it was when Clemens and Katarina met and were later married. This Ball will be a marvelous one. Only the day before yesterday the Princess told me that there would probably be at least 200 people in attendance.

"You cannot imagine how elegant it will be. All the ladies will have on beautiful gowns of silk and brocade, and you young gentlemen will wear knee britches and silk jackets, though I imagine some of the men will wear regular trousers," Magdalene said.

"Will you and father be going as well?" Rudolph asked.

"Of course. Your father will formally present you to the Prince. At that time the Prince will confer the title of Baron on you. That is quite something, you may be sure. Because of the wars, neither Clemens or Heinrich were presented at court in the proper way. Later some documents were sent to each of them conferring the title of Baron on each of them. But you, my pet, will be the first to have things done properly," Magdalene said.

The next day the carriage, which had been ordered the night before, was ready to take Rudolph and his parents into town so that a proper suit, appropriate for court presentation, could be ordered. When they arrived at the small tailor's shop in Mildenburg, the owner, Herr Schneider, came out to meet the carriage. Giving his hand to Magdalene, he escorted her into the shop, offering her a seat close to the window where the light was the best.

"Herr Baron, my esteemed patron, to what do I owe the high honor of this visit?" Herr Schneider said as he gently rubbed his hands together. At the same time he stuffed in his side pocket the tape measure which had been around his neck.

"Ah, my dear fellow, Herr Schneider, I want you first to meet my son Rudolph, for he is the honored one today," Friedrich said.

"It is my privilege and pleasure to be of service to any member of the House of Damsgaard," Herr Schneider said, bowing first to Friedrich and then to Magdalene and Rudolph.

"Thank you for being willing to see me today," Rudolph said, who returned the bow.

"You see, Herr Schneider, my son is to be presented to the Prince in about a month at the Spring Ball, where he shall be elevated to the peerage as a Baron. We must have a suit of the finest brocade for the occasion," Friedrich said with a flourish of his hand in the direction of Rudolph.

"Let me bring you some bolts of cloth which you might find attractive for so important an occasion. Please, won't you be seated around this small table. Do you have any colors which you would prefer?" Herr Schneider said, turning to Rudolph.

"I think dark blue would be most attractive," Rudolph said, glancing at both of his parents for their concurrence. They both nodded.

Several bolts of different shades of blue were brought out by one of the apprentices. After seeing and feeling several examples, a rather bright blue was selected.

"Herr Baron, I believe your son has very good taste. No doubt he has been well schooled by his parents. Now I think we need to take proper measurements. If the young gentleman would come with me, we can obtain the measurements at once," Herr Schneider said. The two of them went to a small area in the rear of the shop where measurements were taken by the apprentice and recorded, all under the critical eye of Herr Schneider.

While they waited, Magdalene said to Friedrich, "It's hard to think that so soon another one of our sons will be making his way in the world."

"It does seem like only yesterday that Rudolph was chirping away in his cot. Soon Eduard and Bertha will be coming here for their presentation fineries as well," Friedrich said.

"We will need a fitting in two weeks, if that is convenient," Herr Schneider said as he and Rudolph returned to the front of the store.

"Yes, of course, that will be quite fine, Herr Schneider. We are pleased that you have been able to meet our needs so well," Friedrich said as he and Magdalene rose to leave.

The Spring Ball, scheduled for May 2, 1822, would be the biggest event of the principality since the yoke of Napoleon had been cast off. For Rudolph and the several other young people from the area who were invited, it would be an important occasion and one which would be remembered for many years to come. It also meant that these young people could expect to have many doors opened for them in all matters relating to their future occupations and marriages, which their parents understood, and in time, they too would understand.

Preparations for the big event were much in evidence in many of the homes of the principality and at the palace of the Prince and his court. It was the Prince's intention that the renewal of the Spring Ball should signify to everyone that good times had returned and that expectations for the future would be vastly improved. In all there were to be 10 young women and 10 young men to be especially honored. A few other eligible people had also been invited as they had not been officially recognized at court at an earlier time due to the uncertainties created during the Napoleonic Wars.

For several days both Magdalene and Friedrich coached

Rudolph on just how he was to approach the Prince, when he should bow and how he should respond to certain questions. Everything had to be carefully choreographed and rehearsed so that no mistakes would be made.

On the appointed night Friedrich's coach, which had been made ready early in the afternoon, was brought around to the drive about 7:30 P.M. Magdalene descended the steps, resplendent in a pale blue taffeta gown with a headdress which was fashioned from white ostrich feathers. Standing on one side of the staircase was Rudolph in his well tailored blue brocade jacket and black knee pants. On the other side of the staircase were Bertha and Eduard, who had been permitted to see this spectacle first hand, imagining, no doubt, the day when they would be the center of attention. At this point Friedrich emerged from his study wearing his special deep maroon silk jacket and lighter breeches. In addition he had his ceremonial sword at his left side. To Magdalene he offered his arm and together they went to the carriage, followed by Rudolph, handsome in his plumed hat. He turned to wave to his brother and sister and they in turn smiled and waved to him from the top of the outside steps. For his part Rudolph felt some apprehension but this feeling was largely overcome by eager anticipation, of wonderful events.

As they drove up to the grounds of the palace, they observed that several other carriages had already arrived. Even now the passengers from Baron von Willebrandt's carriage were being helped up the lower steps of the palace. Each carriage in turn was managed in the same fashion with the grooms taking the carriage around to a nearby field that was used for such occasions and where they could be retrieved at the end of the evening.

Actually Rudolph had only once or twice before been in the palace, but he had been so well rehearsed that there was no looking around as to what one should do next. Friedrich and Magdalene made their way up the grand staircase to the cloakroom, a long corridor lined with various animal trophies which the Prince or one of his ancestors had shot and mounted. Candles were lit even though there was still much light coming in from the windows lining the cloakroom on the side facing the courtyard. Several other dignitaries who were present bowed in recognition of Friedrich and Magdalene. Rudolph quickly glanced at the young women to see if any struck his fancy. All of the young women wore pastel colored ball gowns, some embroidered more elaborately than others. They had been carefully coiffured, and many had flowers woven into their hair.

Toward eight P.M. the Lord Chamberlain came to the door of the throne room and tapped his cane three times. At once the talking subsided, and the first of the young ladies and her parents moved to the door. Each of the presentations took only a few minutes. The guards opened the throne room door as the Chamberlain approached. Soft music could be heard as the door opened. It abruptly ceased when the heavy gilt door was closed behind the family being presented on the other side.

Eventually it was time for the von Damsgaard family to be presented. Magdalene turned to give Rudolph a quick squeeze on his hand, and she offered her most radiant smile. Rudolph's heart had begun to race, but he carefully followed his much rehearsed instructions and felt completely confident. The Chamberlain called out his father's name, and they approached the Prince, bowing. The Prince, seated on his magnificent throne, waved them forward.

"We are delighted, Herr Baron, that you and the Baroness have graced our house this evening," the Prince said as he motioned them to come forward. The Princess smiled and gently fanned herself with her large ostrich fan.

"My family and I are honored that you would receive us this evening, Your Highness," Friedrich said in response. Friedrich moved slightly to the left and Magdalene to the right of the throne area.

"You honor us by bringing your son to court," Prince Franz said. He motioned Rudolph to come forward.

Rudolph bowed and came forward, kneeling before the Prince who then rose and took the sword provided by the Chamberlain. Friedrich turned to the Prince and said, "If it pleases Your Highness, may I present my son Rudolph Thomas Oscar,"

The Prince placed the sword on Rudolph's left shoulder and then his right. "Honored one, hereafter you shall be known as Baron Rudolph Thomas Oscar von Damsgaard.

Please rise, Baron, so that everyone may see you," the Prince said.

Rudolph rose, bowing first to the Prince and Princess, then to Friedrich, then Magdalene, and finally to the courtiers who were assembled. He turned again to the Prince who placed a scarlet ribbon with a medal of his family's coat of arms around his neck.

"I am deeply grateful to Your Highness for this high honor, and I pledge my eternal loyalty to you and your house," Rudolph said in a clear voice. He backed away, bowing as he left, and was followed by his parents, who also bowed until they reached the opposite side of the throne room. As they raised their heads, all of the others in the room clapped gently. Once more Magdalene squeezed her son's hand.

Now another young man was being presented in the same fashion, and so it went until all of the young men and young women had been presented and honored. The Prince and the Princess then rose, and the throne room doors were opened as they approached. The Chamberlain stood at the door and announced, "Ladies and Gentlemen of the Court of Ostend-Aachen, their Royal Highnesses, the Prince and Princess, request your presence in the dining room." An immediate shuffling sound resulted as the several parties moved towards the throne-room doors and then filed into the banquet hall off the lower courtyard.

The banquet was more formal than Rudolph had ever seen. Place cards had been arranged so that the young men and women honorees were arranged to provide opportunities to become acquainted. Rudolph found himself next to an attractive young woman by the name of Mlle. Melanie Schlager. Before the dinner began, Bishop Kuttnauer provided a suitable, but long winded blessing, asking for health health, happiness and prosperity for all of the assemble nobles of the land. Rudolph found his dinner guest to be most pleasant. "How does it happen that we've never met before?" Rudolph said.

"I rather imagine it was because Napoleon forbade it!" Melanie said. Her deep brown eyes were twinkling as she said this, and she fanned herself in the manner of young ladies of proper grooming. She was wearing a light yellow gown, adorned with small blue bows. Her dark brown hair was arranged in a pompadour, with small combs strategically placed to keep every strand in exactly the proper position.

"Yes, I'm sure you're right! But now that the Emperor has gone, we can put things right. Tell me where is it that you live?" Rudolph said.

"We live near Humboldt in a section known as the 'watches.' I think our family has lived there for 50 centuries! Don't you think that is impressive? And what of you?" Melanie said.

"To be sure. I think my ancestors were all Vikings and probably were raiding the coasts of Britain and France at some point. Apparently they tired of that and decided to settle in Jutland and then moved all the way to Ostend-Aachen. But, I say, do you know when the dancing is to begin?" Rudolph said.

"Mama was a bit vague when I asked her that question, so I guess I cannot help you very much. Why do you ask?" Melanie asked.

"My brother says I'm an incurable romantic. If that's true, I'd like nothing better than to ask you if I could have the first dance whenever that is to be. May I have that honor?" Rudolph asked.

"I quite agree that dancing will be a delightful diversion. I find all of this presentation formality to be rather tedious. Yes, Herr Baron, I would be happy to accept your kind invitation," Melanie said, blushing slightly.

"Thank you very much, but I would rather you'd call me by my Christian name of Rudolph. This Baron business is a bit new to me and certainly too formal for anyone who is my own age," Rudolph said. As the various courses of the dinner were served, Rudolph and Melanie continued their animated conversation, each finding the other to be quite attractive.

At the conclusion of the dinner, the Prince and Princess rose and led all of the courtiers to the ballroom, which was the same as the throne room. The two of them sat down, and the Prince then waved to the orchestra conductor, and the music began with a formal waltz. All of the young people knew that this was a 'passing in review', but most of them found the opening dance to be much more of interest than all of

the other festivities of the evening. Certainly Rudolph and
Melanie were quite captivated by this feature. As they danced
past Magdalene and Friedrich, Rudolph said, "Those are my
parents. Now show me where your parents are located."

With a few more turns they were passing close to
where the Schlagers were standing. "With the next turn you
will be almost face to face with my father and my mother is
beside him, wearing a pink gown," Melanie said.

Although Rudolph danced with several other young
women during the course of the evening, he kept coming back
to Melanie over and over again. Towards the end of the evening
Melanie and Rudolph were introducing their parents to each
other. Everyone seemed delighted to meet each other.

"Perhaps you would be so kind to come to Langford
Crossing in a fortnight," Friedrich was saying to Lord Schlager.

"Of course. We would be honored," Lord Schlager said.

"Wonderful. I'll write the details in the morning,"
Friedrich said.

Around two in the morning, some of the guests began
to leave, and the von Damsgaard family moved down the grand
staircase to the receiving area where their carriage was waiting
under the portico.

"Rudolph, I found Mlle. Schlager to be quite charming.
Such a beautiful gown and did she not dance quite well?"
Magdalene said to Rudolph as they rode together.

"Yes, Mama, Melanie is charming and someone whom I
should like to know even better," Rudolph said.

"I feel certain that can be arranged," Magdalene said. To
herself she thought, this young woman would make a lovely
wife for Rudolph. Although he's still underage, but time, after
all, passes swiftly.

Within a fortnight or so an afternoon coffee was
arranged by Magdalene. It was a beautiful warm day late in
May. Close to the appointed hour the Schlager coach could be
seen from the small hill on the north side of the farmland. Not
wishing to seem too aggressive about a match which was not
the least bit certain, Magdalene and Friedrich were dressed in
rather ordinary clothes. Nonetheless, there was an air of
excitement among the staff, who knew something important
was at hand so the house and gardens had been cleaned and

decorated.

Early in the afternoon Rudolph proffered an invitation to Melanie that they should make a small tour of the property. She willingly accepted, and with parasol in place they soon wandered along one of the lanes towards the forest which was on the north side. "Rudolph, I am so happy that your mother has arranged this opportunity for us to come to your home. Did we not have a great evening at the Prince's reception?" Melanie said.

"I thought it was capital, Melanie. You know I was rather dreading the whole affair, but it seems this is something one must go through at a certain age. Mama says it means coming of age. I don't quite understand what that's supposed to mean as not everyone has such opportunities or requirements of fancy balls," Rudolph said.

"Yes, I suppose not everyone has the same things in life. It always seems in Europe that we have a lot of fighting. M y father says Napoleon almost made us French for a period of time, but what a silly thing that is as almost no one I know can speak more than a few words of French," Melanie said.

"It is rather silly. Now the French have a new king, though he is from the old Bourbon family, I believe. Of course, you always have to wonder in these parts whether it is better to have the French at your door or the Austrians or now the Prussians. I rather like our little country, don't you?" Rudolph said.

"Yes, I do. Do you ever wonder what you will be doing in 25 years? Melanie said.

"No, not too much. You see I hope to go to a University such as Heidelberg, where m y brother is now studying," Rudolph said.

"Lucky you! That sounds rather exciting. What would you study?" Melanie said.

"I want to learn all about forestry. I think it is a crime that so much of the land is now being devastated b y logging all over Europe. I think it should be preserved somehow. But I'm sure this must bore you, Melanie. Perhaps we should return to the house," Rudolph said.

"I suppose we should, but what you say is not boring at all. I am interested in learning more," Melanie said.

While the young people were absent, the two families became better acquainted, and each family learned something of their recent pasts. The day seemed like a success to Magdalene, who could not help herself when it came to making matches for her children. Many more contacts presented themselves over the next few years, and Melanie and Rudolph grew closer and closer to each other.

CHAPTER 8

Joy and Sorrow

The ravages of war having been swept away, all of Europe seemed to be prospering once again. Rudolph did go off to Heidelberg, following Heinrich's footsteps, but he selected a forest management program. Not long after his return to Ostend-Aachen, he was given a royal commission to be the assistant overseer of the Prince's forests. In this capacity he worked directly with his father who was both Overseer and the royal Exchequer.

This new status provided Rudolph with a handsome stipend and much authority to carry out his plans for the conservation of the forests, a topic about which Rudolph had developed strong convictions. He had witnessed the sharp reduction of many of the forests in several of the German states as they raced towards building their new cities, using timber as well as coal for fuel in ever greater quantities to supply the needs of the emerging factories of the cities, especially those along the Rhine. In addition, large quantities of timber were sold off to the Scandinavian countries and to the British. The hardwood forests were declining, he thought, at an alarming rate.

Not all of Rudolph's waking moments were taken up with his official duties. Finding time to become well acquainted with Melanie was a great joy in his life. It was during the Christmas holidays of 1829 that Rudolph and Melanie confided their love for each other. On the day after Christmas Rudolph asked Baron von Schlager for his daughter's hand in marriage.

"My esteemed Herr Baron, as you know, I have become very fond of your daughter, Melanie, and we have declared our love for each other. With all my heart and soul I humbly beseech you to permit me to marry Melanie," Rudolph said.

"I cannot say that I am surprised by your request, Herr Baron, but, come, let us take a glass of sherry to offer the proper toasts!" Baron von Schlager said. Going over to the bookcase, he returned with a salver on which were two glasses and a decanter of sherry. After pouring out two glasses and handing one to Rudolph, he raised his glass to the young suitor.

"I salute both you and my daughter, and as I give you my blessing for your intended betrothal, I wish for you the greatest health and happiness. You may be sure that our family looks forward to being linked with yours."

"I am deeply grateful to you for this approval of my intentions. I can hardly wait to become a part of your family as well. May we call in Melanie and her mother to share in the news?" Rudolph said as he took a sip of the fine sherry.

"By all means," Baron von Schlager said. He opened the door to the hall and, as anticipated, his wife and daughter were sitting on either side of the archway. On seeing him, they quickly moved to where he was standing in the doorway, pretending they had no knowledge of what had just taken place within the library. The formality quickly vanished as Melanie rushed into the room and fairly jumped into Rudolph's arms.

For a time the two just stood there with arms clasped about one another, though shortly they glanced about to take in the approving eyes of both of Melanie's parents.

Plans had to be made between the two young people and their respective families. Though Melanie and Rudolph were ready to set the marriage date within a week, a suitable date could not be made quickly, so that it was not until mid-July of 1830 that the wedding took place. Since both families were predominantly Protestant, the wedding was held in the Evangelical Church, with Pastor Hermann Niemueller officiating.

One of the legal matters which caused some delay in setting a date was obtaining the Prince's permission for the two to be married. Two or three visits to the court had to be completed, and, even though Rudolph had a small office in one wing of the palace where he carried out his official duties, several official documents had to be completed before approval could be given.

Among some of the other details to be worked out were such matters as a dowry and also a suitable tract of land to be obtained from Friedrich and a house to be planned. With Melanie at his side the two walked over the land which was to be theirs to determine the portion best suited for building a house. Not surprisingly, they were given no end of advice from both sets of parents on this matter.

Meanwhile the fortunes of Europe were being changed once more following the death of Napoleon. The French had allowed another Bourbon, Charles X, to be crowned, but a small revolution in 1830 removed him, and Louis-Phillippe, of the Orleans branch of the Bourbons, was crowned to take his place. One of Napoleon's legacies had been the breaking down of the authority of the European aristocracy. The small German states carefully tried to replace as much of the old authority as possible, but it was never again to be as it once was. With an expanding Prussia on the east and to some extent on the west, a restoration of the monarchy in France, the small states like Brunswick and Ostend-Aachen, remained intact, but their rulers were apprehensive. None of the Princes could imagine what would result from the growing industrialization or the increasing strength of Prussia.

"Mama, there are so many opportunities all over now," Rudolph said one morning to his mother as they sat together at breakfast.

"My dear, whatever do you mean?" Magdalene asked.

"As you know, weaving is now done entirely by machines in England so that the workers only have to guide the thread. Nothing is done totally by hand anymore. And that means there is greater opportunity for making huge profits, as is now happening in England," Rudolph said.

"Yes, I understand something of that sort. It is also happening in France and the Lowlands, but where is the opportunity of which you speak?" Magdalene asked.

"My wish is somewhat different. If the Prince and other rulers allow their lands to be stripped bare of timber, we will find ourselves with a lot of money but only barren, unsightly lands will remain! I must find a way to convince them that unbridled cutting off of the trees must be slowed, if not stopped," Rudolph said.

"Well, my dear, in your new position you ought to be able to do just as you say. Do you have a chance to speak to anyone at court about your concerns?" Magdalene said.

"Only to the Lord Chamberlain and father, but they seem more interested in getting me married than anything else," Rudolph said.

"But, my dear, it is the task of the elder statesmen to

be certain that all details of matrimony are carefully followed, and I, for one, cannot disagree with them," Magdalene said.

"The date is set for July. The von Schlagers will have to work things out with the church and the pastor. I want to get on with seeing that we have a house to live in," Rudolph said.

"Do have patience, my dear! Show me what you have under your arm. I think I see plans," Magdalene said.

Rudolph unrolled the plans which he had with him and using some dishes as weights, he was able to spread them out on the dining room table. The architectural style was similar to the Georgian style of Great Britain with a central hall opening to a drawing room, a dining room and a library. Upstairs there were to be four rather spacious bedrooms.

"Well, this will be quite an elegant house, my dear," Magdalene said.

"Not excessive, I trust. After all, I expect to live for a good many years," Rudolph said.

The year wore on, and the marriage finally took place with great ceremony. By the next Christmas the new house was completed, and what a wonder it was. To have a new home was what both Rudolph and Melanie wanted and needed, as Melanie was expecting their first child. Late in the spring of 1831 Helene was born. Early in the summer young Helene, her parents, and her grandparents all participated in the christening, conducted by Pastor Niemueller in the same church where Rudolph and Melanie were married.

The winter of 1832 was a severe one, and many people were becoming ill. Friedrich developed a severe congestion which did not respond to any of the remedies his doctor prescribed. He would get better and then he would have a relapse. He had periods of intense coughing, followed by choking spells. By March he was confined to his bed and seemed to be getting weaker every day. Magdalene was constantly in attendance, bringing him whatever he wanted, trying to make him comfortable, to no avail. On March 31 he died in his sleep.

Magdalene was devastated to such an extent that she took to her bed, refusing all food and taking only small amounts of tea. Bertha, Heinrich, and Eduard were helpful, as was Rudolph, in working out all of the details for the funeral. The burial was to be in the family cemetery. Magdalene seemed to find new strength as the time for the funeral came

closer. At the gravesite she was the last to leave because she wanted a few moments alone when she threw some dried flowers into the grave, flowers which Friedrich had given her on their wedding day.

Dressed in black, even to the cloak which she had wrapped about her to ward off the penetrating cold, Magdalene leaned heavily on Rudolph's arm as they walked to the carriage. "Oh, Rudolph, what am I to do without Friedrich? He was everything to me," she sobbed.

"Mother, come stay with us for a while, at least until it gets a little warmer," Rudolph said.

"Yes, I would like that for a few days until I regain my strength," Magdalene said. Rudolph arranged for her maid to come along as well, since he sensed his mother would require a great deal of attention.

By early May, Magdalene had recovered her sense of direction and returned to her own house. For a time Heinrich lived with her, having completed his doctoral studies at Heidelberg. He would be taking up a new post at Halle a little later, but for now he was able to be a great comfort and stabilizer for Magdalene.

Magdalene was delighted to be a grandmother again and again. Helene was born in 1833. There was always activity going on in the household of Rudolph and Melanie. Following Friedrich's death, more responsibilities were shifted to Rudolph, some of which entailed legal aspects of the estate.

Since Rudolph was regularly at court, it was easier for him to accomplish whatever had to be done by staying in the family home, for which his mother was eternally grateful. Not long after his father's death, the Prince elevated Rudolph to the position of Chief Supervisor of the Forests. To mark his greater level of responsibility, Rudolph grew a heavy mustache and a goatee.

"Rudolph, I certainly like your new whiskers. They make you look as handsome as any Bourbon Prince and certainly more handsome than any Prussian Prince," Melanie said.

Stroking his whiskers, Rudolph said, "I hadn't thought of my appearance in those terms, Melanie, but I'm pleased that you find them appealing. Do you think van Dyke would like to paint my picture looking this way?"

"Of course he would." Melanie replied. With that she gave Rudolph a kiss on the cheek.

In March 1836 Magdalene received word that Clemens, who had become a high official in the Peruvian army, had died. It seemed that he had been leading a patrol into the high Andes when his horse, apparently frightened by a snake, reared back and threw his rider off the cliff. He died in January 1836 at the age of 46. Although Magdalene once more was overcome with grief, she accepted this tragedy much more readily than Friedrich's death only four years earlier. Magdalene again received great support from Rudolph during her period of intense bereavement.

During the following winter Melanie was again pregnant. One morning she slipped on the ice on her front steps and twisted her knee which caused her to have to go to bed for the last two months of her pregnancy. Maximillian, her second child, was born without difficulty, but Melanie did not recover as she had following her earlier pregnancy. She had some suffered a moderate amount of hemorrhaging at the time of her confinement, which undoubtedly weakened her.

On the evening of April 22 Rudolph was shocked to see how pale Melanie had become. When he went into her room, he found that she was almost as pale as the sheets. She had refused dinner and had taken only small sips of tea during the afternoon and evening, according to Stephanie, who seldom left her side.

Rudolph was beside himself in anguish. He turned to Stephanie, saying, "Help me prop up Melanie." The two of them arranged pillows and slowly Melanie opened her eyes and smiled faintly at Rudolph.

"Sit beside me," she said weakly, but her adoring eyes spoke volumes about her love.

Rudolph removing his boots, coat, and cravat crawled in beside her. For several minutes he held her so that her head rested on his chest. As they sat together, Rudolph began to sing some of the nursery songs which Melanie sang to Helene. Melanie had always been most happy singing, and now she seemed content in Rudolph's arms. He kept singing and humming on and on into the night. She died very peacefully in his arms that night in May 15, 1838.

Rudolph who had been such a pillar of strength for his mother on two occasions now needed her help. Magdalene moved into Rudolph's house to take over the various house wifely duties, not the least of which was looking after the two children.

"Mother, I think I only partially understood how devastated you were when father died. Now I am in the same situation. What am I to do? You can't go on taking care of us this way," Rudolph said.

"My dear son, I am always here for you. You must lean on me now as I did on you. No one knows what God's plan is for us, but I know that for now I can be of help here. We should take one day at a time until we see some light," Magdalene said.

"You're right, of course, but I see no light at this time. My precious Melanie!" Rudolph said, and he repeated his gratitude towards his mother many times. After a few months, Magdalene persuaded Rudolph to obtain a housekeeper who could take over the tasks of organizing the household to make certain that the children had the care they needed.

Gradually Rudolph regained a sense of direction for himself and his family. Frau Huppel was just the sort of person he needed. She was a middle-aged woman whose husband had been killed in one of the Napoleonic wars many years ago. She had one daughter of her own who was now grown, living a few miles a way. Frau Huppel was a well-organized and somewhat retiring woman who knew exactly what to do. Within a few months the household was running smoothly once more, and Rudolph could attend to his forestry work.

Christmas had always been a favorite time of year for both Magdalene and Rudolph. In 1844 Magdalene organized a great party of both old and new friends from the area. Among the new ones was a young woman, a Scottish sea captain's daughter, who had been tutoring some of the children at court who were interested in learning English. Capt. McLeod had married a Brunswick girl, and they had one daughter, Leonora. When his wife died, he began looking for some place to settle down for a time, and eventually came to Ostend-Aachen. Magdalene had met them on a few occasions and invited them to her party. Leonora was a tall willowy young woman in her early twenties, somewhat plain but pleasant. Magdalene wondered whether her son might not find Leonora as pleasant as she did.

Magdalene knew her son well and soon after the Christmas festivities were over, Rudolph began seeing Leonora more and more. When she was introduced to Rudolph's children, she seemed to understand each of them. Without being the least bit overbearing she soon found that she was well liked by all of them. At first Rudolph could not imagine that he could love another woman, but that point of view changed.

Several weeks later when Rudolph was having a late afternoon coffee with his mother, he said, "For all of these years I could not imagine anyone who could take Melanie's place in my heart, but Leonora seems to be very close. Do you think I would be crazy to ask her to marry me?"

"Oh, my dearest son, I think it is not only possible for you to love another woman, but I do believe it would be wonderful for both you and the children. Remember, you are not even 40, so you have many years ahead, years which should be filled with happiness for you. Do follow your heart!" Magdalene said.

"Thank you, Mother. I'm so glad we have talked about this matter, for I have been wrestling with the way I feel for several weeks now. Knowing how close you and I have been with all of our tragedies, I thought I had to talk to you first. Thank you, for listening to me and giving me the uplift I need. Yes, I do believe I am in love again and what a wonderful feeling it is," Rudolph said.

Rudolph let no great amount of time go by. About a week later he wrote to Leonora to see if he might call upon her soon. She promptly returned the message by inviting him to tea one day early in February.

As Rudolph drove up to the quarters which she and her father, Capt. Ian McLeod, shared in the center of town, his mind was whirling.   On arrival Rudolph was immediately admitted into the salon, where he waited for Leonora.

"Herr Baron!   How wonderful to see you again," Leonora said and stretched out her hand to him.   She was wearing a dark brown dress with long, somewhat billowy sleeves with a lace insert in the front.   Rudolph thought she was beautiful in every respect.

"Thank you for seeing me.   Your room is delightfully cozy with the fire in the stove and the pale winter's sun bringing its cheer to every corner," Rudolph said.   The room was not large but had several pieces of carved walnut tables and three chairs.   The bay window with its lace curtains pulled back looked out on the square.

"Do sit down, Herr Baron, and I will have Sophie bring us some tea.   As I have spent more time in England than on the continent, I find that I still prefer tea to coffee.   I do hope you don't mind," said Leonora.   She rang for Sophie.

"Yes, Mum," Sophie said as she entered the room by a side door.   Sophie, a rather heavy set woman with a   pretty face,   gray hair which she had wound about   her head in a series of braids.

"Sophie, would you be so kind as to bring the tea over here by the window," Leonora said.

In a few minutes Sophie returned with the tea tray and placed the dishes before Rudolph and Leonora as they sat at either end of the small tea table   located in the bay window. Leonora carefully poured the tea and passed the cakes to Rudolph.

"I fear my visit has put you to a great deal of inconvenience, Leonora, but I do thank you very much.   It is so pleasant to be in your company, and this lovely room radiates with your charm.   Tell me how are things going at the palace for you?" Rudolph said.

"My young pupils are conscientious in their studies.   I think Maximillian is a bright young lad.   He is learning English much more rapidly than the others and seems anxious to learn, striving hard in everything he does.   Still, the others are also astute but in a different way," Leonora said.

"I wish all of my children could have the benefit of your teaching.   It is so difficult for me to be sure that they are receiving all the instruction they should. Ever since their mother died, they have had to shift for themselves more than I would wish. Being both father and mother is a complicated matter and one which I don't relish," Rudolph said and smiled broadly to Leonora, who caught his glance and returned a broad smile of her own.

Leonora poured some more tea and said, "I know something of what you are up against as my mother died before I was fully grown. Though my father did the best he could, for which I shall always be very grateful, still there are things a young girl wishes she could discuss with her mother."

"Yes, I'm sure you are right. I think of Helene in this regard. She needs some guidance from a woman," Rudolph said.

"Leonora, I have become more than just fond of you as we have come to know each other. I thought I could never be in love again, but I am and I adore you! I love you! It would give me the greatest pleasure if you would consent to be my wife," Rudolph said with words almost tumbling out faster than he could express everything which was in his heart.

"Herr Baron! You sweep this poor country lass off her feet," Leonora said as she picked up her fan and began to fan herself.

Rudolph reached out and grasped both of her hands in his. "I have been thinking about this for many weeks now and I don't mean to overwhelm you, but my love for you is great and sincere. I think I am one of those men who cannot proceed well without a loving woman at his side. And please, you must call me by my Christian name. No more Herr Baron," Rudolph said.

"And I am not one of those women who falters. Yes, dear Rudolph, I will marry you, though you must talk to my father first," Leonora said.

"Leonora, you have just made me the happiest man in the world. Of course, I shall see you father at once," Rudolph said. He moved his chair so he was exactly beside her and gave her a warm embrace and kissed her many times.

Rudolph lost no time in being in touch with Capt. McLeod. The two of them met at the small hotel, the Adler, to talk.

"Capt. McLeod, you know I have become more than just fond of your daughter Leonora," Rudolph said.

"I'm certainly not blind, sir. I have noticed a growing interest on your part," Capt. McLeod said.

"I have spoken to Leonora and she has agreed to marry me if I have your permission," Rudolph said.

"Since Leonora has already confided in me concerning her feelings toward you, I agree to your proposal with the greatest of sincerity," Capt. McLeod said.   Grasping Rudolph's hand, he gave him a hearty shake.

The date for the marriage was set for early December.

Some members of the Court, chief among them the Princess, did not think it was proper for the two to be married, and wrote to Magdalene to that effect, stating that Rudolph was marrying beneath himself and his family.

The wedding,, held in December 1844, was a modest but pleasant affair.   Immediately Leonora brought her considerable organizational abilities and charm to bear on the estate of Baron von Damsgaard. Life began to hum for all of them as a result.

CHAPTER 9

A New Twist

As the new Baroness von Damsgaard, Leonora took her responsibilities seriously. From her experiences at the palace serving as a governess, she knew that moving too abruptly would bring criticism, scorn, and disruption. No new methods for the household were introduced without discussing them first with the appropriate staff and always with Rudolph.

One morning at breakfast Leonora said, "Rudolph, I was wondering what you would think of adding some roses, especially some red climbing ones, on the south side of the terrace?"

"As I recall, red roses are your favorite, so why not ask Dieter to get some and then tell him where you want them planted. I suspect a number of things want fixing up. Over the past seven years I just haven't been attentive to the gardens," Rudolph said.

"My dear, you had a lot of other things on your mind during those years, and I dare say climbing roses, let alone red ones, were not high on your list," she said.

"That's for sure. But I thank you for letting me slip out of my responsibilities so nicely. I do admire how well you seem to have learned all of the routines. It's wonderful to have you at my side, and I thank the good Lord every day for my great good fortune," he said.

"It is I who am most thankful to have a wonderful husband, fine children and soon to have one of our own," Leonora added.

In short order there were three children, Elizabeth born in 1846, Melanie born in 1848 and Karl in 1849. "Motherhood becomes you," Magdalene said one afternoon when she came over for tea with her daughter-in-law.

"I am so delighted to have you say that, for I· have thought many times that this is exactly what I was made for. I love everything I am doing. Rudolph seems content and the two families seem to have meshed well," Leonora said.

"Yes, my dear, your growing family has come together in a most admirable way. Do you know that even the Princess said the other day that she had truly misjudged you. She remarked that few people could have pulled this family together as adroitly as you have.   And, may I say, your mother-in-law loves everything about you," Magdalene said

"Thank you. Thank you. You are generous in your praise. I still try hard to live up to all of those kind and wonderful remarks. Do you know though, I sometimes fear that everything is going so well that it cannot last," Leonora said.

"Nonsense! Leonora, what on earth could go wrong? You must get rid of any such thoughts," Magdalene said.

"Yes, I suppose I do worry too much, especially when everything does seem to be flowing in the right direction," Leonora said.

A few weeks later after dinner one night Leonora said, "Rudolph, is everything all right? You seemed unusually quiet tonight."

"Leonora, you have a sixth sense. Today I had a terrible row with the Lord Chamberlain. He says that the Prince wants to sell all the timber from the forests from here to Mecklenberg. That is a huge area, and I said it seemed unwise to sell off so much of the lumber, which would leave that whole area bare and raw," Rudolph said, becoming more agitated as he spoke.

"That does seem most unfortunate. It would be too bad if all of the lovely forests were gradually eliminated. Where would the wild animals and birds live? What do you propose to do next?" Leonora asked.

"I'm not sure, my dear. I would like to talk to the Prince directly, but that is almost impossible to do most of the time. I do not have the easy access to the Prince which my father enjoyed. Lately I've been given little respect. My comments are quickly cut off whenever I speak at the Council meetings. The state's finances are in good condition, so I don't see why the Prince feels the need for more money just now," Rudolph said.

"Yes, I am sure that is true, but what alternatives do you have?" Leonora asked, looking perplexed.

"That's just the point. Not many, I suppose. I could try to persuade some of the other courtiers on the matter and perhaps the Prince would listen to me if he knew others had a similar opinion," Rudolph said.

Within the next few days Rudolph sought out the Lord Chamberlain, Graf Wilhelm Wohlgemacht. Graf Wohlgemacht was about the only person at court who could always obtain an audience with the Prince. Rudolph wrote a short note asking that he might see him and was in turn given an appointment for 10 AM two days later.

With mounting anxiety, Rudolph knocked on Graf Wolhgemacht's door.

"Please come in, Herr Baron. What can I do for you?" Graf von Wohlgemacht said. He motioned for Rudolph to sit down.

"My Lord, I hardly know where to begin. I have the feeling I have fallen out of favor with His Majesty. No one seems interested in hearing about my opinions. That fact has caused me to wonder about my usefulness to His Majesty and to our country," Rudolph said.

"And what are those opinions about which you have concern?" the Graf asked. He picked up a silver and crystal letter opener which he always had on his desk and began to twirl it in his hands as he kept his eyes on Rudolph.

"I believe your Lordship knows that I think it is unwise to reduce our forests any more than we have. If we and others do not stop, there will be nothing but barren land in all of the north German lands. We should preserve for tomorrow and not squander today what can never be replaced," Rudolph said. As he spoke, he could feel his anger rising, and he detected perspiration trickling down his cheek.

"Herr Baron, His Majesty is being asked to sell timber to build houses, factories, warehouses and even to provide fuel for some of the factories. We feel we must compete with British and French interests. Do you disagree with that?" the Graf asked, looking fatherly towards the man who many considered something of an upstart, perhaps even a firebrand.

"No, certainly not, but if we eliminate the forests we may have floods as they do in the Low Countries and we will have little beauty. Coal provides a good fuel and is being used in England very much now, as well as in the upper Rhine valley and the Ruhr valley. I implore you to accept these ideas of conservation," Rudolph said.

The conversation went back and forth in this fashion

for several minutes. Finally Rudolph said in a petulant manner, "I gather my ideas are of no importance to you."

"My dear Baron, your insinuations are not appreciated. Your father would certainly not have conducted himself in this most ungentlemanly fashion. You seem to be saying that His Majesty and those of us in his government do not know what we are doing. If you wish to remain in the government of Ostend-Aachen, I suggest you immediately discontinue these continuous tirades and decide to cooperate rather than obstruct the desires and wishes of His Majesty and his government," Graf Wohlgemacht said. Having stated his position, he pushed his chair back from his desk and scowled at Rudolph.

"Your Lordship, my opinions are founded on sound scientific principles which I learned as a student at Heidelberg University. I feel I must defend what I believe is correct. I cannot and will not alter my opinions," Rudolph said.

"Baron von Damsgaard, if you are unwilling to comply and, if you do not relent, I must warn you that you risk being dismissed from your positions of Assistant Exchequer and Chief Forester. In addition you may risk banishment from the country. I urge you to think about what I have said carefully. I would remind you that you have twice now presented your ideas to the council, and no one was in agreement with what you were saying. No one was impressed with what you were saying.

"You sound to me like some incurable romantic, totally impractical. I suggest that you give me your answer within 48 hours. Now, if you will excuse me, I have other things which I must do today," Graf Wohlgemacht said.

Rudolph immediately stood up. "I take my leave, Your Lordship," he said. Bowing, he backed out of the Graf's office. On reaching the corridor he walked swiftly back to his own office where he slumped down in his chair and stared out of the window.

When Rudolph came home early that afternoon, Leonora was surprised to see him, as he seldom came home in the early afternoon. "What brings you home so early, my dear?" Leonora said

"Very bad news, Leonora. I have just had a most unpleasant conversation with the Chamberlain. He states that

I probably will be relieved of my offices as Assistant Exchequer and Chief Forester if I do not immediately agree to drawing up the regulations about cutting the timber in the forests. I have 48 hours to comply," Rudolph said.

"How dreadful, my darling! What are you going to do?" Leonora asked.

"I don't know. Right now I need some spirits to settle my brain. Do you care to join me?" Rudolph said. He went over to the cupboard in the library where three decanters were always in readiness. Pouring some whiskey into a glass, he downed it almost in one swallow.

"Rudolph, if the worst happened and you lost your post here, what would you do?" Leonora said. She sat down in a chair facing him, carefully smoothing the folds of her dress as she did so.

"I once said that I would never emigrate to America, but I suppose that is one of the options. Another, of course, is to go to Austria or to Peru as Clemens did some years ago. What I would do in any of these countries is something else again. I understand that one can get a grant of land in some of the sections of the United States. I might see if the Prussians would have me in Berlin. Eventually the Prussians will swallow up all of the smaller north German principalities, I suppose. But I don't want to leave right here.

"Just think of it! I have lived right here all my life and our children have been born here," Rudolph said, becoming increasingly agitated as he paced around the room. He poured another glassful of whiskey and gulped it down as well.

Leonora went over to the side of the room and pulled the bell cord. In a minute Stephanie appeared in response.

"Stephanie, would you please bring us some cheese and bread," Leonora said.

In a few minutes Stephanie returned with a tray of some cheeses and some bread. Putting it on the table next to Leonora, she said, "Will that be all, Mum?"

"Yes, Stephanie, thank you very much," Leonora said. She offered some bread and cheese to Rudolph, who accepted it.

"I'm not much in the mood for eating, but thank you all the same, Leonora. I think it is time for me to write to the

Chamberlain to tell him I cannot go on as things are. I shall draft a letter first and let you have a look at it, since it might need some refinements," Rudolph said.

The letter he wrote started, "Your Esteemed Lordship,

"I have lived for 12 years with the intent of being useful to His Majesty and the State through my knowledge of forestry and to do everything possible to preserve the forests. I had hoped to gain your trust through these efforts. I have stated my opinions and hoped to gain your approval. It is clear that I have been unable to persuade you of the wisdom of preserving our natural treasure, the forests. I have been told that my ideas are unacceptable, though I have expressed what I believe is in the best interest of the court and the people of Ostend-Aachen.

"I have come to the unhappy conclusion that my views and principles (I must be truthful) seem to be too extreme for His Majesty, his government and administration . My ideas convey contrary views. Without a change on your part I cannot see a happy and useful relationship any longer.

"Since I will not bow to prejudice and I do not want to fall victim to weakness, there is little more I can do. I believe public opinion is on my side. I do not know what I can do or say further.

"What I have said already can be misinterpreted, and I would not have anyone, least of all His Majesty and you, to read either bitterness or reproach between these lines. I am calm and be it only the calmness of a wounded deer, the calmness of resignation dwells within me.

"I feel little is left for me. My strength, as well as my trust, are broken like a field of wheat battered by a hailstorm. My eyes are open and with a penetrating look, I can see the past in the present. I see half a century in just one moment, and I realize that anywhere but here should very likely be my country in the future.

"Too proud to bow to the judgment of a world which can neither find my ideas wise nor do what I think is right, I am determined not to lose my self-respect. My high ideals bring me to this conclusion.

"I repeat again that in view of the many demonstrations of lack of confidence in me, the total change of my personal position and the lack of all courteous respect, I do not feel the strength in me to keep on serving, at least not to my own satisfaction.

"Most obediently, I feel obliged to request that you, my Lord, request His Majesty to dismiss me from his service with a suitable annuity. If I had my own means of subsistence and no children, I would not have made this last request. However, this request I nevertheless present, relying on your well-known noble affection for my family, to use your influence which only you have to help me find other employment.

"Most obediently and with deepest respect,"

At first nothing happened. About a month went by, and one morning Rudolph was summoned to the Chamberlain's office, which was only a few doors from his own. As he entered the office, Rudolph had a sinking feeling, one of forboding.

"Good morning, Herr Baron, please sit down," Graf Wohlgemacht said. Rudolph did as he was asked.

"His Highness and the Council have reviewed your petition, and it is with sincere regret that we accept your wish to be relieved of your responsibilities of Chief Forester and Assistant Exchequer. His Highness regrets having to do this. He requests that you relocate elsewhere outside the boundaries of Ostend-Aachen.

"His Highness has authorized that you be given a yearly stipend of 700 talers. Do you have any questions, Herr Baron?" the Chamberlain said as he kept twirling the silver and crystal letter opener in his hands.

Rudolph sat for a few moments staring at the Chamberlain in disbelief. He wondered for a moment whether the Chamberlain would use the letter opener as a dagger and thrust it in his heart. Finally he said, "That's all there is? All my life I have lived here as a loyal citizen of the State of Ostend-Aachen, have served His Majesty for many years, and now I am to be dismissed to live on a pittance in a foreign land? Where is the justice? Your Lordship, is there no appeal?"

"If you will allow me, let me inform you that the arrangements which His Majesty has made are most generous. Not everyone is given these types of opportunities, and this much of a stipend for life," the Chamberlain said.

"But where is the concern for me and my family who have been loyal to this state for hundreds of years? This is extreme, and merely because I dared to state an opinion which was in opposition to some of the members of the court," Rudolph said. He stood up and was pacing back and forth across the room.

"Come now, Herr Baron, calm down. I suggest that you talk things over with your family, especially your wife and mother. Everyone says there are great opportunities for young men your age in both South America and North America.

"I have been authorized to give you a grace period of two months, but at the end of that time there will be a final declaration made, make no mistake about that," the Chamberlain said. With that he walked out of the room, leaving Rudolph alone and dejected.

CHAPTER 10

A Time for New Directions

Although the summer had passed, fine weather continued into the autumn. This year was unusually lovely across the north of Europe. The harvest was mostly completed, and the air was crisp and pleasant. One day in early October 1853, as he made his way back to his estate, Rudolph kept looking out of the carriage window but found no solace in the countryside. His spirits were at their lowest.

When he arrived at the steps, Leonora came to the door. She took one look at her husband and knew at once that something important had gone wrong, She said, "You look very discouraged, my dear. Come into the library and tell me what has happened."

"First I must have strong drink to settle my nerves, Leonora," Rudolph said. Going immediately to the cupboard in the library, he poured himself a full glass of whiskey and drank it straight down.

"Leonora, it is worse than you can imagine. I have been given two months to clear out. It was a terrible session. The Chamberlain, that miserable worm, took great pleasure in telling me that His Majesty would not agree to any portion of my petition. He just suggested that we emigrate to Hungary or the New World. Just like that! And he has offered a stipend to defray the costs in the New World," Rudolph said.

"Is there no one else to whom you can appeal?" Leonora asked.

"No one, unless it is the good Lord Himself," Rudolph said.

"Perhaps the Emperor in Vienna?" Leonora asked.

"For over 40 years the Holy Roman Empire has ceased to exist, ever since Napoleon reorganized everything. No, there is no one for us beyond the Prince," Rudolph said.

"What do you mean by a stipend, Rudolph?" Leonora asked. She had seated herself beside him and held his hand.

"Seven hundred talers a year! Do you know how much it costs to live as we do?" Rudolph said and slumped further down in his chair.

"No, my dear, I really don't know. Is 700 talers such a small amount?" Leonora said.

"It is a pittance! Our costs must be four times that amount and I don't consider us extravagant. Do you see how our status would be altered? We will be paupers," Rudolph said.

"I suppose it would make a difference, but what else can we do?" Leonora said.

"It truly appears that we have no alternative. Have you ever thought of where else you would like to live? Do you know anyone in America, Austria-Hungary or Peru?" Rudolph said, becoming sarcastic and petulant.

"I hear that many German people go off to some place called Wisconsin, in the middle of America I believe," Leonora said.

"I need another drink," Rudolph said and poured himself another tumbler of whiskey.

"I know Max has a map of North America. I'll see if he might bring it to us so that we could all get a better idea of what North America looks like. Perhaps we can locate Wisconsin as well," Leonora said as she went off to find Max.

In short order Max and Leonora returned with a roll of maps which Max had accumulated. Max laid them out on the library table. "Look, Papa, here it is - Wisconsin. And here's Milwaukee, which I understand is where many people from this region settle," Max said.

"What is the name of that big lake?" Rudolph asked, showing minimal interest in the geography lesson.

"I'm not sure how you pronounce it, but it's called Michigan. It is one of five lakes which are all connected from here at Lake Superior over to Lake Ontario and then out to the St. Lawrence River and eventually to the Atlantic," Max said, pointing out the different items as he spoke.

Rudolph studied the maps a while longer. "Ah, here is New York which is where most ships from Europe land, I understand," Rudolph said.

"Yes, that's where most immigrants land, though some now go to California where they've discovered gold. Father, if we're really going to emigrate, why not send me over first to see where we might settle?" Max said.

"Perhaps we should, Max, but I think Leonora and I need to do a little more thinking before we jump in that direction," Rudolph said.

The next morning at breakfast Leonora said, "My dear, if we no longer have any options here, perhaps we should think of sending Max to America to get some facts together about places like Wisconsin."

"Yes, but my brain is reeling.   I really feel awful. Perhaps after some strong coffee, I can think better.

"What a dreadful time to have to think about such things! Just now Europe is once more unsteady.   There have been so many little wars.   So many little revolutions in 1848 - Prague, Budapest, Paris.   These wars have made conditions unstable.   Look what has happened.   We finally got rid of Napoleon and the Prince turns around and makes a treaty with the Prussians, thinking we would be more secure.   We are now included in a confederation of German states, essentially controlled by the Prussians in Berlin.   The Prince can not do anything without consulting the Prussian ambassador.

"But we have to do something. You may be right. Perhaps we should send Max to America to try to get some clarification of how things are there.   Someone told me a few weeks ago that there may still be some free land available there. We'll have to see," Rudolph said.

"Shall I fetch Max so that we might at least get started on our planning?" Leonora asked.

Rudolph gave a long sigh and said, "Yes, do."

When Leonora returned with Max, they found Rudolph poring over the maps which they had used the night before.

"Max, how do you feel about being the advanced guard to America?" Rudolph said.

"It sounds like a great adventure.   What is it you want me to do?" Max asked.

"I think it would be well to go to New York and Chicago and talk to some people there.   Adolph Bittersdorf went there and talked to the land grant people about Wisconsin and Minnesota and some other places.   What peculiar names they have for places in America.   I believe he then went to Milwaukee, where he was told about various places, one of which was Merrimount, if I recall correctly.   Can you think of any name more ridiculous?

"We need to know about costs of land, availability of

land, and, while you're at it, we need to know more about necessary papers, like passports. In the meantime I can find out more about some of these things at the castle. I still know some people there who will talk to me. From this part of the world most people will sail from Bremen, so that is the place to start. When do you want to start?" Rudolph said.

"As soon as I can. Perhaps even by Friday," Max said.

"Good. I'll get some talers for you. You'll need some of those, you know," Rudolph said.

In no time it was arranged that Max would go to Bremen to book passage on the first ship to New York. The new adventure had begun.

About two months later Rudolph received a letter from Max which he had sent from Milwaukee.

"Dear Father and Mother,

"This is an amazing land, so vast. The trip from Bremen to New York was very bad. We encountered two storms which tossed us about a bit. Many of the passengers became seasick, but I was fortunate and was not sick at all. The food was very bad.

"It took me over three days to go by train from New York to Chicago. I went on the Erie Rail Road and the route passes through long sweeps of farm land, through New York, Pennsylvania, then Ohio, Indiana, and Illinois. The land looks very much the same, very fertile I would think, judging from the crops which one sees on many of the farms. North of Milwaukee there is still good land for sale at about 7 or 8 dollars per acre.

"There appears to be some fine housing in the cities but I saw nothing which would compare with what you are used to in the smaller communities. In fact some of the housing is very primitive, rather like that used by peasants in Germany.

"For the most part people are very friendly and they do seem ready to help with advice and information which newcomers need. The people do not seem resentful of one's being European. Many people speak German very well, though everyone also speaks English, which essentially is the official language in the United States.

"I have made a small payment to hold some land near Merrimount. There is a small village close by where I easily contracted for about 160 acres. An acre is smaller than a hectare, as you know. It has a small house on the land, which could easily be enlarged. I have taken an option on this property which must be settled within four months.

"I shall start back to New York and thence to Bremen and be home in a few weeks. I trust this letter finds you both well.

"Your devoted son, Max."

When Max returned in a few weeks, both Leonora and Rudolph peppered him with questions. "Now, Max, are there still many Indians about when you get away from the big cities?" Leonora asked.

"Well, they say there are some, but mostly that's further west. You see one or two in some of the cities. I saw a couple of drunkards in Chicago, but the Indians don't seem to pose a problem any longer. I understand that there are some in the far north of Wisconsin," Max said.

"Max, you said in your letter that you made a small payment on a little land which had a small house on it. How small a house was it?" Rudolph asked.

"Well, Papa, compared to this house, it would be rather small. There is a kitchen, a front room or parlor as they call it, and two bedrooms. That's it. But it is a well-built house and would be a place to start. Most of the houses in America are small except in New York, where I saw some larger homes," Max said.

"How dreadful! How can anyone expect us to live in such a hovel?" Rudolph said.

"It's not a hovel, Papa, but it's not a mansion either. I think one could at least be comfortable there. Incidentally, I rather liked Milwaukee and could think of living there," Max said.

"Leonora, what do you think? I really need a drink now," Rudolph said and went to the cupboard to pour himself a tumbler of whiskey. After a moment he was calmer.

"Rudolph, my dear, I think it is better to have a roof over our heads than nothing, which is about what we will have here," Leonora said.

"Yes, yes, you are right, but I still find it impossible to think of leaving right here. After all, I was born here and all of my children were born here as well, and I love the forests. It all started with that blackguard Napoleon, then the Hapsburgs and now the Prussians. Such turmoil. Belgium splits off from the House of Orange! I see nothing but continuing conflict and change. One day we will be part of a greater German empire, dominated by the Prussians," Rudolph said.

"Rudolph, we must make some decisions. If we are to leave, we must decide what to take and where to go when we arrive in New York," Leonora said.

"Do not push me any more tonight, my dear. I fear I have taken too much whiskey this night and cannot think clearly. Perhaps in the morning we will work out what has to be done," Rudolph said.

As Rudolph stood up, he was quite unsteady, to the extent that Leonora had to link arms with him to get him to the stairs. Together they slowly made their way upstairs to bed.

CHAPTER 11

New Directions

Leonora had arisen early but allowed her husband to sleep longer, as it had become quite clear to her that without a good rest, he would be unable to make the necessary decisions. Stephanie followed Leonora into the bedroom and placed the breakfast tray on the stand near the window where Leonora often had her breakfast.

"Rudolph! It's time to have a bit of breakfast," Leonora said as she opened the curtains to allow the morning sun to stream in.

Rudolph groaned and rolled over, making no effort to get out of bed.

"Rudolph, here is a cup of strong coffee. I know it will help you," Leonora said. She placed the cup on the bedside stand and gently tugged at Rudolph to get him to sit up, which he gradually did. As he began to sit up, Leonora propped him up with several pillows.

"Oh, I feel terrible," Rudolph muttered. After taking a few sips of the coffee, he looked about the room and finally got out of bed. Putting on a dressing robe, he came over to the table by the window and sat down opposite Leonora.

Looking out on the gardens which stretched before him, he sighed and said, "Soon we must leave everything I love and cherish. Where is the fairness in all of that? Why has our Lord forgotten about us? Have I committed some sin for which I'm being punished?"

"Here, my dear, have some of this lovely brown bread which I know you like. You have always been an honorable man. I'm sure the Lord is not punishing you," Leonora said and placed a covered plate before him.

"Thank you for giving me my favorite breads this morning. It tends to reinforce my dejection to think that I must leave all of this - my home, my country, my life. The coffee has been helpful in clearing my head. Now that Max has given us the necessary information about Wisconsin, and to think that there really is such a place, we must select a date for leaving. We must also think about what few things we can take with us and what must be sold. What ideas do you have? I'm sure we will be limited in how much we can take, as it all has to be shipped at some cost, I would imagine." Rudolph said.

"Perhaps only a few special things like my coffee service and necessary clothes should go with us," Leonora said.

"Yes, yes. The cost will be great. Clothing for us and the four children alone will be a big factor, several trunks, I shouldn't wonder. Max, of course, will take his own things. If possible, I must find a way to take the long case clock which has been in the family for well over a century, but otherwise the sooner we sell off the furniture the sooner we will get the idea in everyone's head that we are, in fact, leaving," Rudolph said.

"Should we set a date in our own mind as to when we want to leave? Will booking passage be difficult?" Leonora asked.

"Probably we should get Max to work out that detail for us. He's really good at that sort of thing. He can go to Bremen and work with the same company he selected previously. I think within four or six weeks at the outside, we should think of leaving. Just think, it will be spring by the time we get there," Rudolph said.

"My dear, have you thought about how we are to let the servants and the workers know about our plans?" Leonora asked.

"For all I care they can just learn about everything on the day we leave!" Rudolph said. He could feel his face becoming flushed as he spoke.

"I know how you feel, but it seems we should give them some inkling of our plans. Some of them, like Stephanie, could obtain other employment," Leonora said.

"Later, later perhaps. We haven't really said anything to our children, but of course, they can guess from what Max must have said," Rudolph said.

"Could you send Max off straight away to make the passage requirements? Once we know that, we can talk to the children about our plans," Leonora said.

"Yes, yes! I'll talk to Max today. He has a good head for these things. Yes, I'll see him as soon as I get dressed," Rudolph said.

Having finished breakfast, Rudolph washed, shaved and dressed. He thought he looked somewhat haggard, with puffiness below his eyes, and he seemed much older. He went down the stairs slowly. Almost every step seemed like an effort to him. A he came to the hall, he stopped before the old clock. It was almost 11 A.M. so he waited for the clock to strike and for the carved figures to emerge from the doors at the top of the clock to perform their dance. When this activity was over, he patted the clock and went to the library, where he sat down in his favorite leather chair. For about 30 minutes, he just sat there trying to think how much money they were likely to get from selling most of their possessions. He calculated that 10,000 talers would be the maximum. Just then there was a knock at the door.

"Come in," Rudolph said and turned towards the door.

"Papa, Mama told me you might be interested in my services as your broker," Max said.

"What? Oh, yes, yes, your mother and I had a discussion earlier this morning - about leaving and making some arrangements to go to Wisconsin. Will you go to Bremen for us? We should try to sail to New York in about a month. My older brother Heinrich will remain at Heidelberg and mother will stay here in Ostend-Aachen. Going with us will be Elizabeth, Melanie, Karl, and, of course, you. We'll have to see about Helene, Otto and their little Paul later, now that she's married. Whenever you get ready to go, I'll give you a bank draft. Find out about shipping trunks and perhaps a few other things like the big hall clock," Rudolph said.

"Papa, of course, I will be glad to do that. I could be ready to go in two days from now," Max said. He then ambled about the library, looking at the books for a time but he kept glancing at his father who just sat almost motionless in his chair.

"You know, Papa, America is not a bad place at all. I rather liked it, as I told you," Max said.

"Yes, I heard you, but what you don't seem to understand is that I don't want to go anywhere, not to Budapest, not to Lima, not to London, not to Berlin and certainly not America! I am being forced to go somewhere I don't want to be, and no one can seem to understand that. I can't have anywhere else what I have here," Rudolph said, scowling.

An adventure in the new world appeals to me," Max said.

"Perhaps when I was 22 as you are, I would have thought so as well. But I'm an old man. Try to understand that, if you will. Do go now and make the arrangements," Rudolph said. He turned his back on Max and went to the cupboard to pour himself a glass of whiskey. He quickly drained the glass and sat down in his chair again.

When it was time for dinner, Leonora came into the library and found Rudolph sound asleep, slumped down in his chair. She picked up his glass, which had dropped to the carpet and gently shook Rudolph. "Come, my dear, it is time for dinner, and we have lovely fresh trout already to be served," she said.

Gradually he awakened. He struggled to get up out of his chair to such an extent that Leonora had to help him to his feet. She took his arm, and slowly the two made their way to the dining room, where everyone else was already seated.

At dinner it was their custom to have wine, and Rudolph immediately drained his glass after he sat down. "Go ahead. Start the dinner, Leonora. I may not eat anything. Some more wine, please, Ernst," Rudolph said,

Ernst immediately filled his master's glass. Conversation proceeded at the table, but Rudolph said almost nothing. He sat drinking wine, one glass after another.

After dinner Rudolph returned to the library, where he first poured himself a glass of whiskey and then sat back in his favorite chair, looking out the window. In a short time Leonora joined him and at first said nothing.

"Rudolph, you can't go on drinking yourself into oblivion every night. There are many decisions which must be made if we are to leave within a month or so," Leonora said.

"Really, Leonora, I am not a child. I know we have to do many things, but I simply don't want to do anything. Go along to bed yourself if you want. I will be up later, but just leave me alone," Rudolph said.

In about an hour Leonora returned and found Rudolph on his couch in the library, sound asleep. She covered him with a blanket, kissed him on the forehead and went to bed.

This same sequence of events continued for a few days

until the next Sunday when Magdalene came over for dinner.
After dinner she followed her son into the library and sat on
the couch next to his favorite chair. "My dear, I think I can
help you with your arrangements for going to America. Would
you like that?" Magdalene said.

Startled, Rudolph paused for a moment as he looked at
his mother and then rose and walked over to the window.
"Mother, I'm not a child any more. What prompts this
question?" Rudolph asked.

"Of course, you're not a child, but consider, there are
times like when someone dies, and it's hard to know what to
do with their personal possessions. You're in something of the
same situation. You know you have to get rid of many things,
but there are too many of the old memories around to make
that anything but an agonizing task. I know because I had to
do just that when your father died," Magdalene said.

"I'm sure you're right, but I don't see how..." Rudolph
stopped in mid-sentence.

"Here's how it works. When your father died, I had
some merchants come in to give me an appraisal of those items
which I could not take with me when I moved into my new
rooms at the castle close. In addition, I have now been
approached by at least two land speculators who want to help
with the selling of your house and the lands that go with it.
Now don't ask me how they knew things might be for sale!

"I would not make any decisions without consulting
you, so you would be informed each step of the way. How
does that sound?" Magdalene said.

Smiling broadly, Rudolph replied, "I might have known
you'd come to my rescue, Mother! When do we start?"

"Tuesday morning. I'll contact the various people and
we'll begin. In that way you can get everything done and meet
all your deadlines. Now stop fretting!" Magdalene said as she
got up and went over to the window where Rudolph was
standing. She linked arms with him and gave him a kiss on the
cheek.

"Very well, that all sounds fine. I suppose you know
Max has gone off to Bremen to book passage for us for
sometime within the next month ," Rudolph said.

"Yes, I had heard," Magdalene said and squeezed his

hand. "Now look, it's all going to work out. Since I am staying here in my house, I can keep an eye on everything for you."

True to her word, Magdalene contacted various vendors and land merchants. It appeared that there was good likelihood that, all told, the property and possessions would bring in about 50,000 talers, which was four times what Rudolph had expected. One evening about two weeks later, Leonora and Magdalene sat with Rudolph around his big desk in the library. Magdalene explained all of the possibilities which she had written out. They decided on von Scoy and Blaupunkt to do all of the work. "Mother, I am most grateful to you for all of t effort you have made. I don't know what we would have done without you at this time. By the way, Max has booked passage on the *Fortuna*, sailing from Bremen early in May," Rudolph said.

"Let's have a bit of brandy to conclude all .of these arrangements," Leonora said. She quickly went to the cupboard and returned with a tray with three brandy snifters and a bottle of brandy. "Here's to our new home in America," Leonora said and lifted her glass to the others. Both Magdalene and Rudolph returned the toast.

CHAPTER 12

Final Preparations for Leaving

"Of course, I wish I could take everything. So far I have written down that I must have the old clock, my gun, the dueling pistols and some clothes. What about you, Leonora?" Rudolph said as he sat at breakfast with her.

"I suppose it will be that we chiefly take clothes and money. I'm sure there is no point in taking many dishes, perhaps a tea set. One can obtain cooking utensils, I'm sure, in America. The children will probably want a toy, a book, a doll, something personal, but otherwise it's going to be clothes for them as well. Rudolph, I like the old clock, too, but it's going to take up a lot of space. Are you quite sure that you want to take it?" Leonora asked.

"I suppose you could say it's my personal toy. I've lived with that clock all of my life, you know. I remember when I was a little boy, I would sit and watch the figurines dance at the different hours. It may be one of the better things to demonstrate to our children our link with Europe. They won't have much else you know," Rudolph said.

"You're right. I think I might take the portraits of my parents for the same reason. The days are going by swiftly, and we need to be packing instead of talking.

"I'll ask Max to get someone to crate up the clock. I think we have enough trunks so that we won't need any new ones. Should we ask him to make reservations for lodgings in Bremen for a day or two in advance of the sailing?" Leonora said.

"Yes, I think we should plan to have at least two, perhaps three, days in Bremen. The dates for sailing are not always correct, you know," Rudolph said.

For the next few days the house was in continual turmoil.

"Mama, why can't I take my doll house to America," Elizabeth asked one morning.

"I know how much you love that doll house, but we are limited for space. Let's look to see which dolls you want to take with you," Leonora said.

Just as one crisis was being solved, another wouldarise. Leonora had told all the servants about leaving two weeks ago. Many tears were shed, promises to write were made, and Leonora wrote many letters of recommendation for each one who wanted one.

In the midst of the trunk packing Max arrived with Hans Eckhardt, who had been retained to crate the clock. He had brought some lumber with him to fashion into a crate. First the clock had to be disassembled, and each piece - the figurines, the weights, the music box, the pendulum and the top bonnet - were all placed on the dining room table on which old sheets had been laid to protect the finish. As this project was going on, Rudolph followed his every move, to be sure he understood how the clock would be reassembled once it reached its destination in America. Hans now set up the saw horses just outside and began to cut up some of the lumber to fashion a crate of the proper size and strength.

Once the container was completed, Rudolph made a list of each piece of the clock as they were carefully wrapped in cloth and then old papers. About half way through the process Rudolph said, "Hans, couldn't we put my rifle in the box as well? It could go along the edge."

"Yes, Herr Baron, we can do whatever you want. I thought you might have some other items to add so I made the box a little larger than it needed to be for the clock alone," Hans said. The rifle was then wrapped in the same manner and placed in the crate.

"My wife has some tea things which she wants to take. Would there be room for them?" Rudolph said.

"Yes, of course. Fetch the tea items, and I will place them inside the case of the clock. That will give it greater strength and be a good place for the tea things as well," Hans added.

"Rudolph returned with Leonora, both of whom carried some pieces of the tea and coffee service. Hans continued his work methodically, and then he hammered on the top. Max and Hans carried the box to the entry hall, where it remained until the final day when things were put in the dray for the trip to Bremen. After Hans left, Rudolph said to Leonora, "It looks just like a coffin. It might well be my coffin one of these days."

"Come now, Rudolph, you must get over these

frightening thoughts. After all we hear about how successful many people become in America, I'm sure there is no reason to feel it will be otherwise for us," Leonora said.

"It would be wonderful to think so, but here we had everything we could want, and America is a strange place for all of us. Why we barely know any English, any of us. I confess I don't know how you can remain as cheerful as you do. It's your life that's changing as much as mine," Rudolph said.

"I have my bad moments as well as you, but I must keep a brave face for the children. They will be the true inheritors of life in the New World. You know I keep wondering whether your oldest daughter Helene and Otto will want to settle in America as well. They really have not said so to me. Have they spoken to you?" Leonora said.

"No, neither Helene nor Otto have said anything definite to me, though I have assumed that they would eventually decide to come along as well. I think Mueller is not so keen on the idea," Rudolph said.

Two days later Helene and Otto came by for afternoon tea. Up to now they had been living in the village not far from the castle where Mueller had secured a position as assistant to the bailiff at court. "Mueller, have you decided whether you and Helene will be coming with us to America? The time grows short, but, of course, you could always come later if you do not wish to come with the first wave," Rudolph said.
168

"Papa, Otto and I have been giving this matter a great deal of thought, and we have just come to a decision," Helene said and turned to her husband.

"Yes, we have. We think it sounds like a great opportunity and we look forward to the trip. Do you wish to have us in the first group?" Mueller said. Otto Mueller was a handsome and rugged young man who often talked about how much he would rather be outside doing whatever needed to be done than to have anything to do with jobs which kept him in an office. "I think it is just the place for a man like me."

"I think it would be easier for all of us to be together," Leonora said. Rudolph nodded his head in assent.

"Remember, we will be leaving here about April 27 in

order to get to Bremen by the 28. Max is making the inn accommodations now," Rudolph said. Helene and Otto left shortly after these announcements had been made and confirmed.

Rudolph continued to be disconsolate to such an extent that Leonora did most of his packing for him. Every evening Rudolph ate little for dinner but he always had two or three glasses of whiskey before dinner and several glasses of wine at dinner. On numerous occasions he slept on his couch in the library. As the end April rolled around, the children had all come to think of the journey as a great adventure. The excitement was high for everyone, even to some extent for Rudolph.

Max had arranged for the dray to go on ahead as it was a much slower moving vehicle. Just before the family was gathering outside to get into the carriages which had been procured for the trip to Bremen, Magdalene arrived from the village in her carriage. Rudolph was shocked to see her dressed all in black, even to a black parasol.

"Mother, it is sad enough to have to leave you and everything that is dear to me, but it is not a funeral. Why do you come dressed in that fashion?" Rudolph asked.

"Rudolph, please do not excite yourself, for you have a long trip ahead of you. I frequently wear black, as you know, ever since your father died. Now I want a big hug and kiss from all of you," Magdalene said. She then busied herself hugging each of the grandchildren in turn. To each one she gave a small gift which had been carefully wrapped. It turned out that most of them received writing portfolios except the youngest children, who were given a small toy.

When it was time for Rudolph and Leonora to get into the coach, Magdalene clutched both to her and kissed them many times. Finally she pulled back and waved them off as they drove down the carriage way. Leonora and Rudolph had watery eyes but the children were all caught up by the adventure unfolding before them. Helene seemed the most wistful of the group, but that mood passed rapidly as the carriages moved out into the main road and headed for the train station where they would board the train for Bremen.

Many hours later, the train came to a stop in Bremen

close to the Hotel Post, a small inn located near to the railroad
station. Leonora had seen to it that everyone had a small valise
to be used for the short stay, making it unnecessary to bring
their large cases and trunks into their rooms. Only Max had
been to Bremen before, and he insisted that they should eat
dinner that night in the old Rathaus close by.

"Do you know, Mama, the Rathaus is over 400 years
old, and the Ratskeller has one of the best dining facilities in all
of the north German states," Max said.

"But, Max, we have never taken the children to any
restaurant before. I'm not sure we could manage everyone,"
Leonora said.

"Mama, things are going to be different now. Helene
and I can manage the children, and you and Papa can just enjoy
the fine dinner which will be served," Max said and smiled
broadly.

"Yes, Max, I know things will be different, but your
father has never taken well to public places," Leonora said.

"I know, but leave him to me this time," Max said.

Max went to where Rudolph was standing looking out
of the window of the hotel lounge. "Papa, do you know they
have the very best beer in all of the north country at the
Ratskeller here? I do suggest we give it a try. Helene and I will
look after the children while you and Mama can relax for the
evening," Max said.

"What, what? You want us to go to the Ratskeller
tonight? Well, I suppose we must go somewhere. Yes, let's go
at once. Do get the children to come along, Max," Rudolph
said.

The Ratskeller proved to be just right for
everybody. Helene, who was used to helping with the younger
children, shepherded them into the Ratskeller, where they were
at a table by themselves. Max and the others had made
arrangements for the beer to be brought to them at once.
Rudolph could feel the tension leave him as soon as he had a
few swallows from his mug of beer. Surrounded by the men of
the family, Leonora began making some plans for the next day.

"Max, why don't you and Papa go out in the morning
to see about the final arrangements for the sailing time. Helene
and I will take the children out to the marketplace and take a

look at St. Peter's Cathedral. Does that sound reasonable, Rudolph?" Leonora said.

"Very reasonable, my dear, very reasonable. I might like to come with you to the Cathedral. You know the famous "Judgment of Solomon" mural which dates back to the early 16th Century is in the Rathaus. We should see that as well," Rudolph said.

Early the next morning Max and Rudolph set out to find out about the sailing. They learned that the *Fortuna* would be sailing at high tide the next afternoon.

"Yes, Herr Baron, your staterooms will be ready for you. I think you will find your accommodations much to your liking. The wagon with your trunks has arrived, and we have them carefully covered by the quay," the bursar said, tipping his hat to Rudolph as he did so.

"Thank you. My family and I look forward to being with you for the trip. Is it six weeks for the crossing?"

"Yes, Herr Baron. This is a seaworthy ship and we should make New York in about six weeks. At this time of year we usually have the smoothest crossing," the Bursar said.

Having learned of the details and having paid the remaining passage which amounted to 50 talers a person, Rudolph and Max returned to the hotel. Everyone had a question to ask. Rudolph held up his hand to call a halt to all of the chattering. "We have the rest of the day to ourselves and tomorrow up until one or two in the afternoon. All the boxes and baggage have arrived and will be placed in the hold of the ship tomorrow. Now we should see the sights of Bremen. Are you ready?" Rudolph said.

Happily it was a mild day so that no one had to wear heavy outdoor clothes. Soon they were out of the hotel and into the marketplace. "Children, look at the statue of Roland. You know that statue is over 500 years old. People here say that as long as the statue stands, Bremen will be a free city," Rudolph said.

"Papa, who was Roland?" Elizabeth asked.

"He was one of the great generals under Charlemagne. So he goes way back to before 800 AD, my love," Rudolph said.

After touring the magnificent cathedral, the family went

to the Rathaus to see the 'Judgment of Solomon' mural. As they grouped themselves around the mural, Rudolph remarked, "Let us hope that the good Lord will judge us fairly and provide a safe crossing of the great sea."

CHAPTER 13

New York at Last

The morning of May 2, 1852 broke fair. A few small clouds floated by, but the sky was a deep blue. The mere contemplation of the departure caused every one to be more than a little excited. One or another of the children would run to Leonora to ask whether it was time to set out for the ship. Everyone was quite ready to go down to breakfast, but, when it came time to eat, most of the appetites seemed jaded as each had their own private thoughts about the unknowns lying ahead.

"Finish up all of you. It'll soon be ten o'clock, and we must be ready for the carriages to pick us up," Leonora said.

With this admonition, the children scampered back to their rooms to be sure that last minute objects were packed in the valise each one would take on board the ship. Overseeing the final packing, Leonora went from room to room to be sure her instructions were being carried out. Meanwhile Rudolph gazed out of the window, wondering over and over again how they would live once they were in Wisconsin.

When Leonora completed all of the checking, she assigned one of the older children to look after one of the younger ones. Close to 10 o'clock she gently linked arms with Rudolph, who was still standing by the window, and softly said, "It's time to go, my dear."

The carriages had drawn up in front of the hotel and, like the skilled general she was, Leonora made certain that all cases were present and that each of the pairs of children were properly ensconced. Only then did she and Rudolph get into the carriage. The trip to the quay where the *Fortuna* was docked took no more than 15 minutes. Once there, the process of checking on everyone started all over again. Max and Rudolph made their way to the bursar's office, where they learned that the departure time would be at one o'clock sharp and that everyone should plan to get aboard around noon.

As soon as the gangplank was put in place, Max and little Karl were the first to get aboard. The bursar's assistant directed all the passengers to their staterooms. The *Fortuna*, one of the newer class of ships, had both sails and steam.

Max said to Karl, "We must go up on deck to see

them cast off the ropes so we can sail down the Weser River."

All the passengers were on deck as the time for sailing was at hand. At exactly one P.M. the ship's whistle gave a mighty blast. This sign was followed immediately by the stevedores on shore who were casting off the ropes, which were promptly pulled up, and the ship began to move towards the middle of the river. Everyone was waving to someone on the shore.

Once again Leonora made her rounds to see that everyone was accounted for and that the older children were paying close attention to the younger ones in their charge. She then went to where Rudolph was standing alone towards the bow of the ship. "It's quite a sight, isn't it?" she said placing her arm around his waist.

"Yes, Leonora, it really is. You know, I find myself rather excited, though sad at the same time," Rudolph said.

By late afternoon they had come as far as the mouth of the Weser and then into the estuary which seemed several miles wide. Soon they were in the North Sea. Max holding Elizabeth by her hand, pointed out the changing landscape. "Look, Elizabeth, we will soon be passing the Netherlands and on into the English Channel," he said.

Sometime after six P.M. Leonora made her rounds again, reminding everyone to get cleaned up for their first dinner aboard ship in 30 minutes. Not surprisingly, the cleaning up was done in record time. Once in the dining room all nine were seated at a large table. By now the ship was moving faster, and a gentle rolling set in so that Melanie asked, "Mama, my bread keeps rolling off the plate. What should I do?"

"The best thing to do is just eat it, and then it won't get away from you," Leonora said.

As the ship progressed into the English Channel from the North Sea, they could again see the coast line, this time of the Netherlands. The shore looked like a ribbon of green, as by this time of year most of the leaves were out. Interspersed with the green would be some cliffs of white chalk. When the Captain announced at breakfast that later the Channel Islands and the northern coast of France would be visible, Leonora said, "I've always wanted to go to the Channel Islands since that's where my mother came from."

Leonora and Rudolph wandered out on the deck as soon as breakfast was over. Now they could dimly see the coast around Le Havre. "Look over there, Leonora, there's France where Napoleon used to hold sway. You know I think everything bad which has happened to us can be traced back to the Napoleonic times," Rudolph said.

"That's quite interesting. What do you mean?" Leonora asked.

"Perhaps many people would not agree, but, as a result of Napoleon's invasions of Italy, Spain, and the German states, the need for more raw materials increased manyfold. When Napoleon was trying to get control of the German states and Austria, the nobility were forced to put up greater amounts of money in exchange for their semi-autonomy. Remember when he established the Grand Duchy of Baden Baden? That was a farce, as it was totally controlled from Paris. That was true for our Prince. All he had were large tracts of timber to offer, and he sold them, despite my counsel to the contrary. Of course, when I refused to change my position, I was ushered out of the mainstream," Rudolph said.

"You know, my dear, much of that history happened before I was born so I don't have such intense feelings. Surely now as we are on the verge of a new life, we can put aside some of these old animosities," Leonora said.

'You're right, but it doesn't alter the fact that we wouldn't be here if we weren't forced by circumstances which neither my father nor I had any chance of altering," Rudolph said.

As the wind quickened, the motion of the ship became more pronounced. By evening several passengers had become seasick, including Otto and Helene.

At dinner that night Helene remained in her cabin. "Poor Helene is feeling very badly tonight," Otto announced.

"Otto, you look none too sturdy yourself. Is there anything either of you would like?" Leonora said.

"Thank you, I can't really think of a thing unless you can command the waves to subside. I'm sure we'll survive as countless others before us have. I will just take Helene a little tea. The truth is, that's about all I want as well," Otto said.

Having obtained a few tea items from the chief steward, he returned to his cabin.

For most of the remaining voyage Helene kept to her stateroom, eating only a few morsels from time to time. Towards the end of the voyage the weather had warmed considerably, and many days aboard ship were pleasant so that Helene, leaning heavily on Otto's arm, remarked, "Otto, I was beginning to curse my ill fate for being on this ship, but I feel enough better today to make it all seem not so bad after all."

"That's good news. Another bit of good news is that the Captain says we are four or five days from New York," Otto said.

"Yes, that's very good news. I tell you, Otto, I think I will never want another sea trip, no matter what the cause," Helene said with a faint smile.

"I can't imagine why we would want to have another trip. You know your father is remarkable. He has complained every day about how bad things are, at home, here, and what is yet to come, but he looks more robust than ever," Otto said.

"He does look quite well. I think he's not been drinking as much on this trip as he had been and perhaps that has helped him," Helene said.

Two days later the Captain announced at breakfast that land had been sighted. He described how the ship would follow the North American coast line and enter New York harbor in a day or two. Most of the passengers began to scan the horizon often during the day.

On the morning of July three the New York harbor was sighted. Word spread quickly, and in no time most of the passengers had come out on deck to watch. The sails were furled so that the ship slowed, but she continued to glide into the inner harbor and by noon had docked on the east side of lower Manhattan. Great cheers rose from the passengers once the ropes were secured to the dock.

Leonora again made certain that everyone was accounted for and that the younger children had someone to look after them as they made their way to the lower deck and out on the gangplank. It was quite warm, and most people were perspiring considerably. Rudolph had on his heavy greatcoat which he quickly removed as he began to mop his brow.

"A truly warm reception we have in America," Rudolph said.

"Yes, I don't know what I expected, but here we are. Our new home!" Leonora exclaimed.

All the foreign nationals who were emigrating were now lined up to present their passports and then be checked by the public health officials to see if they were healthy enough to be admitted. This process took over three hours. By then most of the baggage had been unloaded and was ready to be claimed as soon as their owners had been examined by the health officials. Max quickly organized matters and arranged for a dray to pick up all of their cases and boxes. He had made arrangements for them to have lodgings at the New Century Hotel, only a few blocks from the dock on Maiden Lane.

CHAPTER 14

The Journey to Wisconsin

Leonora sat up in bed, looked around and, noticing the wall clock, determined that it was about half past seven. She glanced over to the other side of the bed where Rudolph was still asleep.

She slipped out of bed and walked over to the window. Down below there were already many carriages and wagons in the street as well as some intrepid souls who were walking along the sidewalks. Looking about the room, she located all of the luggage which had been stored there from the night before. Their clothes were heaped on top of the luggage.

Having dressed, she went out of the room and took the elevator to the lobby. There she inquired in her imperfect English, "Would it be possible to send up breakfast to our room?"

"Of course, Madam. Will it be for two?" the desk clerk asked.

"Yes, two," she said and held up two fingers to make certain the message was clear.

Only two or three other people were in the lobby. Leonora ignored them and returned to their room. "Rudolph, I've ordered some breakfast for us and I think it will be here in about 25 or 30 minutes," Leonora said.

Rudolph moaned a bit and turned over. When the knock came at the door, Leonora opened it to admit the waiter who wheeled in a table and then left. Leonora went to the bed and shook Rudolph who opened his eyes and then sat up in bed.

"How thoughtful of you to order breakfast," Rudolph said and accepted the cup of coffee which Leonora offered him.

"I didn't bother to see if the others were up since I thought we needed a head start," Leonora said. Rudolph nodded in agreement as he buttered a roll.

They were only just getting underway with breakfast when there was a knock at the door. Leonora opened the door, and Max stepped in. "You are early birds, it seems. I was just going to the lobby to see what might be available for breakfast," Max said.

"Oh, Max, I just thought we couldn't face going down

for breakfast so I ordered enough for two. Would you and Helene get the children up and take them to breakfast? I'd so appreciate that," Leonora said.

"Max, you're a great help. What would become of us without you?" Rudolph said.

"I'm happy to oblige. When we're all done, I'll come back to see what our next steps should be. I think we could get a train out this afternoon if you want," Max said.

"Yes, please do," Rudolph said and went on eating.

In about an hour Max and Otto returned for further instructions. Among them they decided that a day to get caught up would be preferable to trying to leave that afternoon.

"Max, I think we need to exchange tallers for dollars. I believe I saw a bank around the corner," Rudolph said. He opened his wallet and gave Max a large amount of money.

The day went by quickly. Some wanted to just walk about the area of lower Manhattan, but others preferred staying in their rooms. At dinner time Max announced, "I have all of the tickets to go on the Erie Railroad, and we leave at 10 o'clock in the morning. Papa, I have arranged for a wagon to take all the baggage ahead of the rest of us, and everything will be loaded for the trip to Chicago. We have to change trains there before we go north to Wisconsin."

On the following morning Leonora and Max were clearly in charge and made certain that no heavy overcoats were left behind and that special toys were tucked under eager arms. When they arrived at the station, Max checked on the boxes and luggage as Rudolph and Leonora herded everybody on board. After they found seats for everyone, they became aware that many of the other passengers were also newly arrived immigrants and were headed to places called Erie and Cleveland, as well as Chicago. Many passengers were German speaking, so they quickly learned the stories as to why they had left Europe. Some had been victims of religious persecution. They all hoped to find peace and prosperity now that they had reached that strange and awesome land called America.

Rudolph remained glued to the window by his seat. "This river must be what they call the Hudson, Leonora. It rather reminds me of the Rhine with its high bluffs," Rudolph said.

"It is easy to see why New York has become such an important sea port. Max says that New York will be as important as Bremen and Hamburg so far as shipping is concerned," Leonora said.

"Yes, it's quite a river and rather pleasant countryside. You notice that not all of the trees have been cut down," Rudolph said.

The train trip became more and more tedious as time went on. As best they could, the passengers, most of whom were immigrants, managed with little sleep and only periodic food which they had brought with them. The first major stopping point was Buffalo. Most everyone got off the train and milled about in the station. The whole stop was over an hour. Some baggage was unloaded for those who were not continuing while stacks of new baggage took their place.

Helene was much intrigued with Buffalo, having learned that Niagara Falls was not far away. "Otto, perhaps we can come back here one day and see the falls. I hear that many newly wed people come here on their honeymoons," Helene said.

"I'm sure it would be quite spectacular, but I don't know what we would do for money just now," Otto said, as he circled the station for about the 20th time.

Following the shore line of Lake Erie, the train headed westward. Since the tracks were fairly clos e to the water, they all marveled at the size of one of the great lakes. The next major stop after Cleveland was Toledo, and again almost everyone got out to stretch and have a look at the surrounding city.

"The names of the cities are so interesting. When I hear Toledo, I think of Spain and not America. I wonder how it happened to get its name here. And that place just before, Sandusky. What a strange name," Leonora said.

"Yes, it is somewhat strange. It probably was an Indian name. I understand that a lot of the American cities were Indian settlements at one time and then were named for them after the European settlers took over," Rudolph said.

"Now the next major stop is Chicago, is that right?" Leonora asked.

"Yes, Mama. Then we change trains for Milwaukee. Not so very much farther," Max said, who was sitting in the seat across the aisle from where Leonora and Rudolph were seated.

"You rather liked Chicago when you were here before, didn't you, Max?" Leonora said.

"Yes, it's already a very important city at the lower end of Lake Michigan and with the manufacturing taking place, it should become even more important," Max added.

The countryside was now flat, with a few gentle hills to the south, and this type of landscape continued on into Chicago. Because of train schedules being infrequent going north, it was necessary to stay overnight in Chicago. Max had again made advanced reservations to stay in a small hotel, the Hotel Meridian, near the station. Boxes, valises and tired passengers all disembarked and were happy to be taken to their hotel where most everyone collapsed from the weariness of nights on the train with little sleep and meals which were often brief and unsatisfying.

In the morning they would take a new rail company from a station on the north side of Chicago. The enthusiasm which everyone had for the trip when they left New York had given way after four days, to exhaustion and boredom.

CHAPTER 15

New Home In Wisconsin

As they looked out of the rain-streaked windows going north from Chicago, the flat countryside of farms and woods stretched to the horizon. The houses and barns appeared to be well constructed and neat homesteads were matched by well cared for farm land.

Max had grown quiet as the train lumbered along. He was slumped in his seat, trying to get caught up on sleep before the group would arrive at Michilac. The others, never having been there before, watched the countryside. Rudolph for the most part stared straight ahead.

"Max says that most of the villages along here have been named for old Indian settlements," Leonora said, speaking mainly to Helene.

Just then the conductor came through the car announcing, "Next stop Michilac!" Max sat up, retrieved his suitcase from the overhead rack and motioned to the others to get their belongings together.

When everyone was assembled on the platform, Max said, "We have to get another cart tomorrow to look over the property, which is about five mile to the west, but for tonight I have reservations for us all at the Adler Hotel, right across the street.

Rudolph placed Leonora's arm in his, and together they made their way across the street. As they walked, Leonora kept glancing behind her to be sure that everyone was accounted for and that Max had made certain that all of the baggage had been collected.

Entering the small lobby, Rudolph announced to the clerk in German, "Baron und Baroness von Damsgaard kommen." The clerk responded in German with clarity, which impressed and pleased Rudolph and Leonora. When Max arrived, he confirmed the arrangements, and the clerk rang a bell to summon a porter to help with the baggage.

After entering the room, Rudolph slumped into a chair and said, "Here we are, my dear, in the New World. Max has some plans for visiting the property so we might as well wait until he joins us to learn what happens next," Rudolph said.

"We can contact the estate agent at any time, and he

will take us to the property I have told you about. The trip is not very far and we can be there in not much more than an hour. Do you both want to go?" Max asked.

"If you are not too tired, Mama, you might want to go with us. Helene and Otto can mind the rest here, I'm sure," Max said.

"Rudolph, Max, I'm not tired in the least. As this is where we will spend the rest of our days, I'd be only too pleased to go with you. Imagine living on a farm!" Leonora said.

"Good! Then I'll see if I can locate the agent, and we should go off first thing in the morning," Max said and left the room.

"I have great difficulty thinking of this place as being home, Leonora. I know that I should, but in every respect things are so strange, so foreign," Rudolph said.

"To be sure, it's different. Look out at that lake, Lake Michigan, I believe they call it. Why, it's as big as an ocean. For the sake of the children we must make the best of it. They will probably adjust better than we, I should think," Leonora said.

About an hour later Max returned to say that he had made arrangements to leave the hotel around 10 o'clock on the next morning. "I've hired a buggy for the two of you, and I will ride along with the agent on horseback. I've also located all the trunks and boxes which are being stored in the basement for the time being. By the way, the agent's name is Mr. Hochmeier, and he knows German quite well. It seems most of the people here are from German states or Austria. German is still taught in the schools, he tells me. Incidentally, we can have dinner tonight at seven o'clock. Does that sound convenient?" Max said.

"Yes, Max, all of that is wonderful and you have really been our savior in seeing us through this wilderness," Leonora said. Rudolph nodded in agreement.

Not long after breakfast, Max showed up with Mr. Hochmeier. All the children came out to the front of the hotel to see them off and stood waving until the buggy was out of sight. Max and Mr. Hochmeier were in the lead on horseback while Rudolph followed in the buggy. As they left the outskirts of Michilac, they picked up a narrow, dirt road leading west. Just as they had been told, they came to a crossroads village called Highland Corners. Mr. Hochmeier, a small, ruddy-faced man in his early thirties, tethered his horse in front of a small one-story building with a sign over the door saying Land Office.

Max and Mr. Hochmeier waited in the road until the buggy drove up. Mr. Hochmeier helped Rudolph and Leonora out of the buggy and said. "Here it is, folks, Highland Corners. The land we talked to Max about is not more than five minutes from here and is 160 acres, mostly cleared of trees."

Both Rudolph and Leonora looked around. There was no sign of any habitation, so it was difficult to imagine exactly where this land might be. Leading them into the office, Mr. Hochmeier motioned for them to sit down and placed a large map in front of them. "The land I'm talking about is right here," he said and pointed to a small plot of land which had been marked off with some hatch marks. "All you have to do is sign a few papers and it's yours. Let's take a look."

Everyone got up and resumed their ride to the area which had been pointed out to them on the map. Just on the other side of some trees was a small four-room house which appeared to be in satisfactory condition. "Mr. Hochmeier, why don't you show my father the land, and I'll show my mother the house," Max said.

As Leonora and Max walked over to the house, Max said, "The land appears to be good, but the house is quite small. Many people add on to houses like this."

"Max, we can manage, but I am very worried about your father. He has become more and more morose and, of course, he is drinking far too much for his own good. This house is not much larger than his library back home. He will need a great deal of help," Leonora said.

"I know, Mother. It will be hard on him, and there is much to be done. Of course, I'll stay for a time. I have no definite plans, but how will you manage? There is only the fireplace for cooking and altogether only four rooms," Max said.

"I think I can adjust, Max, and I'll do my best with your father, but just now I'm worried, though I can't entirely say why. He's always lived well and with servants. Where does one purchase seeds or livestock, I wonder?" Leonora said.

"If you have money, there's no problem, I'm told," Max said

"Whenever there's money, there's no problem. We don't know exactly how much the Prince has set up as a pension for your father. How much will this land cost us?" Leonora asked.

"Everything is in dollars, of course, and I don't know how the gold translates. We must locate a bank in Michilac. You know there is a small school not far from here where the children can attend. Did you see it as we came to Highland Springs?" Max asked.

"Do you mean the little brick building which looks like a small church?" Leonora asked.

"Yes, that's it. I understand that one teacher manages all of the children at whatever age and ability they have. It looks as though father and Mr. Hochmeier are coming back," Max said.

Leonora and Max walked out to meet them. Rudolph was frowning and said nothing at first. He walked into the little house with Leonora behind him. "It's small, but I can manage, my dear," Leonora said.

Rudolph grunted but said nothing until they were outside. "What needs to be done next, Mr. Hochmeier? he asked.

"If you like what you see, you've only to sign some papers stating you will live here and improve the land for the next five years. We can do that at any time," Mr. Hochmeier said.

"That sounds very reasonable. M y wife and I will talk things over at dinner tonight and then we'll be in touch with you. Will that be all right?" Rudolph asked.

"Of course, I believe Max can find the way back, and he knows how to reach me in Michilac. I am at your service," Mr. Hochmeier said.

"Yes, I will lead our little party back. We may drive around a little before returning to the others. Thank you for being of such great service to us. Would the Michilac State Bank be a good place for my father to deposit some money?"

Max asked.

"Yes, that's a fine bank. You'll find the banker, Mr. Hauser, to be cooperative. I'm sure Baron von Damsgaard will find him quite agreeable. I'll be available any time in the morning," Mr. Hochmeier said and bowed slightly in the direction of Rudolph. Rudolph touched his beaver hat and then took Leonora by the arm and led her to the waiting buggy.

For the first few minutes they rode silently and then Rudolph said, "What on earth will become of us in that dreadful place, Leonora? It is such a far cry from what I talked to you about before we were married. How can we all live in that doll's house?" he said.

"My dear, we are alive and well. Others have done the same. In America things are different, but we will learn together. Max said he will stay with us for a time to help get some of the farm things underway," Leonora said.

"Can you imagine what our parents would think of this place? I suppose if I had agreed to all of the awful things the Prince wanted me to do, we could still be in our fine house. How will I face the children when they come to understand how stupid I was?" Rudolph said.

"My darling, you did what you felt was right and honorable, and you can always be proud of that," Leonora said.

"Indeed! Honor! Can one eat honor? Does honor provide you with new clothes? To think that as a Baroness you have to be a scullery maid. No, it's all too degrading. I feel wretched," Rudolph said.

"Come, now, it's not that bad. Let me help you wherever I can. Did you notice the little school house as we drove down. Max says one teacher handles all the children from these parts," Leonora said.

"It's not the Academy where Max and the others went to school. What do we know about the teachers or what they teach, for that matter?" Rudolph said as he held his head and rolled it from side to side.

"You're right. There's a lot we don't know, my dear, but we shall have to learn about these things later. Here comes Max. We must think about going back to Michilac," Leonora said.

"Well, it's different but not impossible, wouldn't you

say?" Max asked rhetorically.

"It's awful. We have no choice but to stay here and see what happens, I suppose," Rudolph said and glowered.

"Father, you're not obliged to stay. We could go further west or to the south. Across the Mississippi there is much land waiting to be developed, I hear," Max said.

"I dare say we could go elsewhere. But what's the point? Nothing we have seen or heard about compares to home in north Germany. No, you've got us started here so we might just as well stay. But I don't have to like it," Rudolph said.

"Father, I agree. Let's head back, for there are papers which have to be completed before you can move to the farm," Max said.

It was early afternoon by the time they returned to the hotel. All the children were waiting for them and showered them with questions about their new house and their new farm.

"Leonora, do answer their questions. I fear the ride has given me a dreadful headache. I simply must have a nap before attending to anything else. You are so much better than I with the children. I must have a glass of wine before resting," Rudolph said. He bought a bottle of wine at the hotel and made arrangements for two bottles of whiskey to be sent to the room.

By the time Rudolph woke up, it was late in the afternoon. He straightened his clothes and went to find the others. Everyone was in Helene's room and, as soon as he entered the room, everyone swarmed over him, asking questions about whether they could have a pony, a sleigh, new clothes, and on and on.

Rudolph tried to put off answering all the questions and said, "We will just have to wait some more. We have to get situated first, and then we need to see if we have any money. Now Max and I must go sign some papers with our estate agent. Mind your mother, and, when we get back, perhaps I'll know more about some of those questions," Rudolph said.

Max had made arrangements for Rudolph to meet the head of the Michilac State Bank, and there he opened an account with some of his gold sovereigns. Later they went to the estate office of Bridley and Hawkins and drew up the papers which had to be completed for the ownership of the 160 acres. Later they would register the deed at the courthouse. Essentially Max did all the talking, and Rudolph did the signing.

On returning to the hotel, Rudolph, with Max's help, planned a lavish dinner to commemorate their new acquisition. When the whole family was assembled, Rudolph proposed a toast, "My dear family, let us thank almighty God for bringing us safely to the New World where we will all begin a new life.

"To my dear wife, I wish to give my special thanks for her constant reassurances and faith that everything would work out. To Max, we are all indebted for his initial and continuing help with every detail of this momentous change. To all of you younger children, may you prosper as new flowers in the spring garden," Rudolph said and drank a full glass of wine which he immediately followed with another.

Somehow Leonora and Helene had found clean clothes for everyone so that their collective appearance was impressive. At one point, as the evening was drawing to a close, Rudolph said to Leonora, "We must show these people how nobility behaves, and you have certainly dressed everyone with that in mind, for which I am deeply grateful."

CHAPTER 16

Life in Wisconsin

In a few months a new way of living began to emerge. A section was added to the house within the year so that there was a separate kitchen, two bedrooms, and a library/living room. Rudolph was eager to see how some of their special furnishings like his old long case clock had survived the move. His pleasure at seeing it in this new house was without bounds. For days it was all he could talk about.

Leonora and Max were both anxious to have a vegetable garden so that they could reduce food expenditures. In time they retained a local farmer, Mr. Trauerknecht, to help with the simple plowing and planting.

"This country still seems very peculiar, don't you think?" Rudolph said to Leonora one night as they were having dinner.

"In many ways I find it a beautiful land with almost endless possibilities, but I suspect that's not what you mean," Leonora replied.

"No, not exactly. While in town today getting some farm supplies, some men were talking about California. Now all I know about California is that gold was found there a few years ago, and, of course, some people made a lot of money. Since then, people at the capital in Washington are talking about whether or not they should allow slavery there. So far as I can tell, they want slaves only for the drudgery, but they approved the admission of California as a state with a proviso excluding slavery. In Europe we got rid of serfdom years ago, but people here are still debating about the good or the evil aspects of slavery. Now isn't that strange?" Rudolph said.

"Before we came to America, I was not aware that there still was slavery here, my dear. Only the other day when I was talking to Helene, she said that someone had told her there might be a civil war over this issue. Do you hear anything like that?" Leonora said.

"Oh, yes, that talk is quite common. Even Heinrich Trauerknecht was telling me about that the other day after he plowed up our first field. He says that people in the southern part of the country are becoming much more worried about the prospect of a war. It's certainly ironic that we lived through all of the years of the Napoleonic wars, and then we come here only to find ourselves likely to be involved in another war," Rudolph said.

"I do agree that all of that is very strange. Changing the subject, Rudolph, Helene, and I are taking some English lessons from one of the neighbor ladies. It's Mrs.. Knause who is giving us lessons in the afternoon. I do hope you don't mind," Leonora said.

"Mind? No, of course not. It will be important for both of you. You can help me. I find reading the newspaper to be helpful, but without a dictionary on my knee I miss a good bit. I'll know where to come now the next time I get stuck," Rudolph said.

By late summer the remodeling was completed, and Rudolph, Leonora, and the children moved into the new section. The few pieces of furniture they had brought with them fit well. It also appeared that the first crops which had been planted would yield a reasonable harvest.

Helene and Otto had become increasingly restless by being so much a part of the household. When Helene became pregnant, everyone concluded that they should have a home of their own. Soon they were able to obtain land which was adjacent to that owned by Rudolph and Leonora. Otto was happy with this new arrangement and so was Rudolph.

Otto organized everything well, and he was able to find ways to keep up with the chores of both properties. Rudolph was especially happy as he soon could relinquish to his son-in-law all of the difficult and, therefore, in his mind unpleasant aspects of the work .

Not long afterwards Leonora was also pregnant. In the winter of 1854 Ruprecht was born to Leonora and Caroline was born to Helene. Both of the children prospered and were brought up together most of the time. Helene's older son Paul was always following his father around the farms. The families were gradually settling into the pace of the area. Otto was always talking of future plans, but Helene had become morose.

"Leonora, I have an intense longing to return to Germany," Helene said to Leonora one morning as the two women sat together with the younger children.

"Really? I'm quite surprised to hear you say that,

Leonora asked.

"I suppose it sounds very irrational, and perhaps it is, but I feel I must show Caroline and little Paul what the old country was like, and I have the strongest desire to see grandmother again. I find myself crying over nothing, and I just don't seem to get rid of the idea of not returning," Helene said, crying as she blurted out her story.

"I can understand your wish to do so. I have some of the same feelings, but we are not out of debt and the farm is just breaking even. It's such a long trip and so filled with uncertainties. Have you talked to Otto about this?" Leonora said.

"Oh, yes, I've talked to Otto and he's not interested but said if I really wanted to make a visit, we could do so," said Helene.

"I know you write to your grandmother frequently. She mentions that in her letters to us. Have you talked to your father about the idea at all?" Leonora asked.

"No, I haven't. I suppose he would try to talk me out of it although I think he still pines for the old place," Helene said.

"You are correct on that point, Helene. He does speak about how wonderful it was there, frequently, but we are different. All of our bridges have long since been burned, and there is no returning for either of us," Leonora said.

"I know I must talk to him, but I fear how he will react," Helene said.

Several weeks passed before Helene was ready to talk to her father. On a Saturday night in June when the two families were together, she brought up the subject.

"Father, Otto and I want to make a visit back to Germany someday soon. I feel I must go to see for myself whether I could live there again. You will think me silly to talk in this way, I'm sure, but we have considered that this is something which we must do," Helene said.

"What? You want to return to where there is no future? Have you taken leave of your senses?" Rudolph fairly shouted at his daughter.

"It's not silly. I know you would like to be there if you could, Father, so why should you berate me in this manner?" Helene said as she began to sob.

"Yes, but my life is almost over, and yours is only just beginning. You have two lovely children and a fine husband and a growing establishment here. What you are looking for is fantasy. There's nothing there for you. Has your grandmother been encouraging you to do this?" Rudolph asked.

"No, no, grandmother has been kind to me in all of her letters. She does say that the Prince is much more gracious now than he had been. She says he may even increase your pension," Helene said.

Rudolph turned to Otto and said, "Otto, you and Helene have made a wonderful home here, and you have so much to offer to your young family. You've made a success of farming. Heaven knows where Leonora and I would be without the two of you. Can't you talk Helene out of this madness?"

"I can't say that it's madness at all. Helene is a wonderful person, but she does pine for a look again at what we left. We think of this as a visit only. We will return," Otto said.

"Such an arduous trip to take for nothing. But I suppose if you must, you must," Rudolph said.

"I think that's about it," Otto said. With that, Helene and Otto and their two children left with both Leonora and Rudolph waving to them as they drove off in their buggy. It was as though they had already departed.

Arrangements were made for them to leave by the middle of the summer of 1858. Otto had worked out a plan for Heinrich Trauerknecht to look after the farming for the end of the summer, and he made out a will leaving all the property to Rudolph in the event of some catastrophe. By August they were to leave from New York on the steamship *Austria,* bound for Hamburg.

One evening not long afterwards Rudolph said, "Leonora, it seems lonely without Helene and her children around here."

"Yes, I miss Helene very much. She and I have become close to each other since coming here. In many ways she always seemed like my own daughter," Leonora Said.

"Yes, I know. Now Max is talking about going to

Milwaukee to start up some business there. It's like having your arm cut off to see first one and then another of the children leave," Rudolph said.

Max did indeed leave, but he wrote frequently from Milwaukee on how well his store was progressing. "This is the place for me. I need more city around me than you do, Father. I shall still be able to visit you regularly, which I like," wrote Max.

Late in September, on one of his visits to his parents, Max brought some bad news. "There's a story in one of the Chicago papers that a ship caught fire while at sea and sank. No one seems to be quite sure yet, but it is thought to be the *Austria*. Here is the clipping, father," Max said.

"Merciful heavens, how can this be?" Rudolph said and handed the article to Leonora to read. Leonora burst into tears as she read the account.

"Oh, Max, how will we know for sure about all of this? Everyone was lost at sea, you say?" Leonora said between sobs, and she collapsed on the sofa with her head in her hands.

"Yes, they say everyone was lost. The German consul in Milwaukee has told me he is trying to find out more to be sure. Probably there will be some clarification within a few days, he told me," Max said.

"Poor dear Helene, my oldest child," Rudolph said. He walked around the house with his head bowed for several minutes. Leonora came over to him and together they embraced.

"All of those beautiful children," Leonora said.

Rudolph went to his desk, found his bottle of whiskey and poured himself a glass and drank it down.

"Perhaps this will help the pain. Oh, God in Heaven, what can be the meaning of this? Why these young people?" Rudolph said to Leonora and Max.

"Father, there are no answers. Certainly not now. We must try to adjust as best we can," Max said.

"I don't see how I can adjust, Max. I really don't. It's one thing when an older person dies, but they were so young. Why did they have to go back?" Rudolph said. He kept on drinking more and more of the whiskey. Eventually he became less agitated, but his speech became incoherent.

About two months later Rudolph received an official statement from the German consul about the fire and sinking of the steamship *Austria*, making clear that Otto, Helene, and their two children, Paul and Caroline, had been lost at sea.

Rudolph found himself unable to get started in the morning without first having a drink of whiskey. Often he would have a drink or two during the day and always two or more at night after dinner.

CHAPTER 17

War Comes To Wisconsin

In 1859 a man named Booth was convicted in a federal court of having rescued a runaway slave. The Supreme Court of Wisconsin released Booth, stating that the Fugitive Slave Act of 1850, was unconstitutional. Later the United States Supreme Court reversed this decision.

Right after dinner Rudolph would often read aloud sections of the newspaper to whomever might be remaining at the table. "Listen to this. This John Brown person seizes the arsenal at Harper's Ferry and then is later subdued and taken prisoner. I tell you, these people are fools or crazy or both. That runaway slave business and now this man Brown grabbing government property will drive the country to war sooner rather than later," Rudolph said.

Leonora seemed to understand that when Rudolph became agitated, he would soon be asking for whiskey, so she tried to change the subject.

"I know you can't vote, my dear, but what do you think that new political party, the Republican party, is likely to do?" Leonora asked.

"I have no idea what they will do, though many people think that man Lincoln from Illinois may be nominated for the presidency. There are now more free states than slave states ever since Minnesota and Oregon were admitted, so there is bound to be trouble with the southern states," Rudolph said.

"We've seen war enough in Europe to know what dreadful things happen to people, but the thought of a civil war, of tearing a country apart, is particularly pernicious," Leonora said..

"Indeed it is. But I don't see much to suggest that cool heads will prevail. Of course, I'm a great one to make such a statement, but still, the thought of killing a lot of innocent people is rather too awful to contemplate," Rudolph said.

"Papa, why can't you vote? You're a citizen aren't you?" Elizabeth asked.

"No, I am not a citizen. When I went to the courthouse to be sworn in as an American two years ago, I thought everything was all set, but the judge told me I would have to renounce my title as Baron. I told him I had no intention of doing that. He then informed me that there was no problem, but I could never be an American citizen as long as I insisted on using my title. As long as I pay my taxes, I can remain as I have always been. All of you children are citizens of this country. The early Americans felt that there should be no nobility in this country after they had won their independence from England. I'm not sure they're any better off as a result, but that's not the reason all the same. Karl, for example, will be able to vote when he becomes 21 years of age," Rudolph said.

"Although women can't vote, of course, I could and did become an American citizen," Leonora said.

After Lincoln was elected in 1860 with a wide margin of electoral votes, there was not only no relief, but the newspapers described the agitation which was taking place in the South. "I hear that some of the people in South Carolina are suggesting that they will secede from the Union. We'll see what Mr. Lincoln can do once he's in office," Rudolph said on another occasion.

No one had long to wait. In April 1861 the garrison at Ft. Sumter was fired upon and three days later Lincoln asked for volunteers to put down the insurrection. "I told you they were fools, and so they are! I wonder what they think is going to happen to them now," Rudolph said to Max as they talked about the state of the country

"Some people think that England will come in on the side of the South to preserve their cotton trade, but I think that's rather far-fetched, don't you?" Max asked.

"Max, do fetch me a drink. I can't possibly answer that question without a little whiskey," Rudolph said.

Max went to get the whiskey and gave it to his father, saying, "Here you are, father. Do you usually start drinking so early in the day?"

"I drink whenever I want to, Max. Now what was it you wanted? Oh, yes, something about England, or was it France, coming in on the side of the Southerners. I can't imagine either one of them doing that just now. What's in it for them? France is essentially out of the Americas. Only Africa interests them, and England has her hands full with

India. Incidentally, Max, the stupid Southerners will find out that there is cotton aplenty to be had in Egypt and India. No one will need American cotton very soon," Rudolph said and finished off his whiskey.

Later in the day Max talked to Leonora, "Mother, I seem to notice that father is drinking more and more whiskey. Am I right in this observation?"

"Yes, Max, I'm afraid that you're correct. Ever since Helene's death, he has been drinking continually, it seems. There are times when I can barely get him to bed before he passes out. I don't know what to do," Leonora said.

"Do you ever talk to him about the amount of whiskey he's consuming?" Max asked.

"I tried once, and all I got for my efforts was the candle thrown at me from across the room. Mind you, most of the time he seems quite fine, but at night he tends to talk about Helene and the children, and he becomes morose and drinks some more. I just try to keep him from becoming agitated because when he's upset, he usually wants to have more whiskey or wine," Leonora said.

The war in the country continued with greater fury but was as yet indecisive. Reports grew about the vast number of young men, North and South, who were being killed. These reports made Rudolph more morose. "What a dreadful place we are in. We thought we escaped the stupidity of the Europeans fighting each other all the time, only to find that their descendants continue in the same vein. You know, Leonora, the Canadians outlawed slavery and freed slaves in 1833, and now, of course, many slaves are finding refuge there when they can get as far as the border. Leonora, do fix a glass of whiskey for me," Rudolph said and slumped down in his chair.

When Leonora returned with a glass of whiskey, Rudolph grasped her left hand and tenderly stroked her fingers. "Oh, Leonora, look at your hands! Once they were white and your fingers slender. Now they are callused, brown, and your nails are broken. It's all my fault. This would not have happened if I hadn't been so stubborn, and we had stayed in Germany. What a wretch I am," he said.

"Now, now, my darling, all of that is past history. I do

not regret your decision to come here. It was the right thing to do. Here now, drink your whiskey. It'll make you feel better," Leonora said.

Rudolph quickly dropped Leonora's hand and drank the whiskey straight down. It was a warm summer night and soon Rudolph went out to the privy before going to bed.

When he returned, Leonora rushed up to him saying, "What's the matter, Rudolph? You have blood all over your shirt. She pulled him over to his chair, where he remained for a few minutes.

"It's nothing. I just felt a little sick out there. I think I'll go to bed," Rudolph said. As he stood up, he fell over. Leonora went to him and gradually got him to his feet.

Leonora slowly walked him to their bedroom and then went to get a basin of water to wash him as blood was all over his face. It was not clear what the source of the blood had been. After he was cleaned up, he collapsed into bed.

"Rudolph, something is wrong. Do you hurt anywhere? Is there anything I can get you?" Leonora asked.

"No, no, I'll be all right after I get some sleep," Rudolph said.

Leonora helped him get his clothes off and his night shirt on. Soon he began to snore and with that Leonora took her lamp out to the kitchen. Not long afterwards she went to bed herself.

As was usual, Leonora got up first and went to the kitchen to prepare breakfast. She called to Elizabeth, "Go see if your father is ready for his breakfast."

In a short time Elizabeth returned and said, "I knocked on the door, but I received no answer so I went inside. Father is lying with his face to the wall and when I called him, he didn't say anything," Elizabeth said.

"Thank you dear. I'll see if I can rouse him. Would you get the others up, please. Breakfast is almost ready," Leonora said.

Leonora went into the bedroom and shook Rudolph. When she turned him away from the wall, she gasped, "Merciful heavens, he's dead!"

Leonora wandered out to the kitchen where Elizabeth was finishing breakfast preparations. She slumped into a chair placing both hands to her head.

"Mother, what's happening?" Elizabeth said, turning from the stove to where her mother was seated.

"All of you, come over here," Leonora said and turned with tears running down her cheeks. "Your father is dead." All of the children crowded around, all talking at the same time. By now everyone was crying.

Elizabeth poured her mother a cup of coffee. "Here, mother, you're going to need this," she said.

"Thank you, dear. I don't know what to tell you. Last night your father went outside, and, when he came back, he had blood all over him. I didn't know what to do except to get him cleaned up and put to bed. He seemed fine. You know, I don't think he was ever sick in all of the time we were married.

"I didn't check on him even after I got up this morning. I suppose we'll have to make some funeral arrangements," Leonora said.

"Karl, you and Melanie take the buggy and go over to Reverend Dornemeier at the church and tell him what has happened. He'll probably want to come by to see what we need to do further," Leonora said, wiping her eyes on her apron.

As expected, Rev. Dornemeier came at once to the front door with his hat in his hand. "Baroness von Damsgaard, what dreadful news these two lovely children have brought to me as I sat at my desk reading my Bible!" he said. He rushed over to where Leonora was sitting in the kitchen and bowed before her.

"Yes, Rev. Dornmeier, it is a dreadful situation. Please help me with making funeral arrangements. I hardly know where to begin. He seemed well before bedtime. He came in from outside and appeared to have vomited a lot of blood. After I cleaned him up, I got him ready for bed," Leonora said.

"Yes, yes, of course. Let us gather your family and have a short prayer," Rev. Dornemeier said. Everyone grouped around Leonora, who still sat at the kitchen table.

"Dear Father in Heaven, we beseech you to accept the soul of our departed brother who has left this world to return to you. Bring comfort to his wife and his children as they must now live without their guiding light. We ask it in Jesus' name.

"Do you have a burial plot here where you would like your late husband to be buried? And what are your wishes about a coffin?" Rev. Dornemeier asked.

"We have a small plot to the east of the house which we established when our oldest daughter and her family died at sea. As to the other details, I will telegraph our oldest son who lives in Milwaukee to ask him to work out what needs to be done. I know there are some legal matters, and I will ask Max to help me with these things," Leonora said.

"Allow me to suggest that since young Master Karl is a very good driver, he might follow me into town, and we can go to the telegraph office at the train station to be in touch with your son in Milwaukee," Rev. Dornemeier said.

When Max arrived early that evening, he immediately got started on all of the details for the funeral and the legal matters of their finances. Almost for the first time since she had arrived in America, Leonora felt a kinship with the community. Several of the women of the church, the German Reformed Church of Norwood Corners, came to the house, bringing armloads of food, offering and providing help in all matters.

After the funeral was over, a marble stone was erected which simply stated, 'Baron Rudolph von Damsgaard 1805-1862.' Having no other choice, Leonora assumed control of all the affairs. She always had been capable, but now she moved in new ways, both for herself and for her family.

CHAPTER 18

The First Marriage

At first not much changed. School started again in September. Mr. Trauerknecht helped with the crops as he had done ever since Rudolph and Leonora had lived at Highland Corners. Time changes some things more slowly than others. Children continue to grow and to change more quickly, often more rapidly than their parents might wish.

Elizabeth came to her mother one afternoon after school and said, "Do you realize that I will soon be 17?"

Leonora looked up from her darning, which seemed never to be completely finished, and said, "Let's see, I suppose you will be, my dear. Does that have some significance for you?"

"Really, Mama, for one thing, I will be finishing school this year, and I will probably be getting married soon," Elizabeth said.

"Elizabeth, I understand the first part of what you said, and I do suppose you will be getting married, but I didn't think it would be soon. Is there some nice young man who has asked for your hand?" Leonora asked.

"Oh, mother, don't be so old world! Nobody asks for 'your hand' anymore. I know you are aware of Frederick Harrington, whom I first met in church several years ago. He's been off fighting, as I think you also know, and he has been writing to me, as I know you know," Elizabeth said.

'Why, yes, now that you mention it, I do think I have seen some of his letters arrive from time to time. Is he the one who was at Vicksburg or was that Jeremiah?" Leonora said in a teasing manner.

"Jeremiah is not in the running, Mother. You may as well know that Frederick has suggested to me that we should get married when this dreadful war is over," Elizabeth said.

"You had better pray that the war ends soon and that Frederick survives. The casualties which occurred at Gettysburg are beyond anything I had ever heard of in Europe. My dear, I do wish the very best for you. Frederick would make a very fine husband, I'm sure," Leonora said.

Another year went by, and it was 1865. On a beautiful spring morning in April the children ran up the drive to the house, shouting, "Mama, Mama, the war's over." Karl, who was in the lead, was waving his arms wildly.

"Mr. Elliott received the news while we were in school and then dismissed the class," Melanie added, running along breathlessly. More ladylike than the others, Elizabeth came along shortly to be part of whatever celebration there would be.

"Are you sure? Oh, what wonderful news indeed! This calls for some celebration," Leonora added, trying to clutch all the children at once. Recently Leonora had purchased a small American flag, which she placed in the crotch of a tree at the front of the house, and they gathered about the tree. Karl saluted the flag while they stood there.

"No doubt the soldiers will be returning home soon, wouldn't you suppose, Mama?" Elizabeth said to her mother after the first burst of jubilation had passed.

"Yes, dear, I would think so. That usually happens after wars end. I suspect you'll see your Frederick very soon," Leonora said, and gave her daughter a kiss on the cheek.

The happiness of the land was soon to be shattered as suddenly as it had come when word arrived a short two weeks later on Good Friday that President Lincoln had been assassinated. Leonora had gone into the village when one of the young men at the railroad station came dashing out of the station waving a piece of paper and shouting the devastating news.

"What madness can this be? After all the suffering have people totally taken leave of their senses?" Leonora said to Mrs. Dornemeier, who also happened to be in the village.

"Indeed it seems that way. As though we didn't have enough sorrow with all those fine young men being killed on the battlefield," Mrs. Dornemeier said.

Although the country was reeling from the assassination news, Elizabeth's world brightened considerably when Frederick came home and rode to see her shortly after his arrival.

On the next day Frederick came riding up to the door. Almost as though a sixth sense were operating, Elizabeth had decided to wear a new dress that morning, so when she saw Frederick, she did not hesitate to run out to the road where he was hitching his horse. Seeing her coming, Frederick stretched out his arms, and she ran to him.

"Oh, my darling, can it really be that you are here?" Elizabeth exclaimed.

"Elizabeth, I have imagined this day for the past three years! How wonderful you look, even prettier than I remembered," Frederick said.

"Mama, look who's come home!" Elizabeth shouted. Of course, it was hardly news since Leonora had been watching from the front door and had slowly walked towards the happy young couple.

"Welcome home, Frederick. This is a memorable and wonderful day," Leonora said.

"Thank you, Ma'am. It's a wonderful feeling to be back in Wisconsin. I guess even though I've seen a lot of this country, right here looks the best I've seen," Frederick said.

"I imagine you two have a lot of things to say to each other, but how about some supper with us first?" Leonora said.

"Oh, Frederick, would you stay? That would be truly marvelous," Elizabeth said, smiling as broadly as her face would permit.

During supper all eyes and ears were directed towards Frederick. "Did you kill any of those rebels we heard about?" 16-year old Karl asked early in the conversation.

"Hush, Karl. No need talk about such things at the supper table," Leonora quickly interjected.

"Karl, the war was really awful. You can hear a lot of things about bravery, and there's some to be found, but it's mostly bad. Bad food, bad sleeping, and worries about home. I just can't tell you how great it is to be home and have that behind me," Frederick said.

"I hate to think of you suffering that way," Elizabeth said, as she kept looking at Frederick rather than eating.

When supper was finished, Frederick said, "Elizabeth, if you've some time, perhaps the two of us might take a little walk."

"Well, yes, I have some time. Mama, I can help you with the dishes when I come back, would that be all right?" Elizabeth said.

"Of course, my dear. Now don't worry about the dishes. Just be back before sundown," Leonora said.

Arm in arm Elizabeth and Frederick slowly sauntered down the lane. "What will you do, now that the war is over?" Elizabeth asked.

"It's something I want very much to talk about. I've been asked by the Army to consider a career in the Army. You see, I'm a captain now, and it seems like a good career for me. I want Wisconsin to be my home, but having the chance to have a peace time career has a lot of possibilities. How does that strike you?" Frederick said.

"I hardly know what to say since I'm not very familiar with such things, but if that's what you think would be a good career, why should I think differently?" Elizabeth said.

"President Lincoln wanted to find ways to reestablish good relationships throughout the southern states, and it seems clear that President Johnson will continue the same policy. The South will need to be reconstructed since parts of it were pretty well devastated. Colonel Wentworth, who was my regimental commander, asked me to consider the Army, and, if I said I would, my first assignment would be in Washington, where Army headquarters are located," Frederic said.

"All of that sounds very exciting, Frederick. When do you have to make a decision?" Elizabeth said.

"Perhaps in a month, it's not certain. But what is certain is that I love you very much. I've never stopped thinking of you and about how much I'd want to have you as my wife, Elizabeth. I know I wrote about that, but I guess nothing is the same unless it's in person. Elizabeth, will you marry me?" Frederick asked.

Coming close to him, nose to nose, Elizabeth said, "I wrote you I would marry you and now I'll say it to you in person. Oh, yes, Frederick, I will."

They held each other in a long kiss and embrace. "I can't tell you how long I've dreamed of this moment, my dearest," Frederick said.

"We must tell Mama, Frederick. After you, she's about the most important person in my life," Elizabeth said.

"What's wrong with right now?" Frederick said. He turned about face and, holding hands, they walked slowly back to the house. When they returned to the house, Leonora was in the side yard bringing in some clothes which had been drying. The happy couple walked quickly to where she was just completing her task.

"Mama, Frederick and I have something to tell you," Elizabeth blurted out quickly.

Looking up, Leonora smiled broadly and said, "I wonder what it is you could possibly want to tell me."

"Mrs. von Damsgaard, I have just asked Elizabeth if she will marry me, and she has accepted, but first I must know if you approve," Frederick blurted out almost without taking a breath.

"Frederick, if Elizabeth will have you, I have no objection. In fact, like all mothers, I am delighted to think one of my daughters is going to be married and to such a fine young gentleman as you," Leonora said. She took both of the them by their hands, pulled them towards her and kissed each in turn.

There was a lot of talking about plans as to when the wedding could take place, but first Frederick had to return to Washington to accept his new position. On returning, he announced that his first assignment would be to Ft. Story in Virginia. Ft. Story was an old fort near Newport, and now after the war it would be rehabilitated as part of the East Coast fortification system which the War Department was planning.

That night Leonora wandered over to the cemetery where Rudolph was buried. She stood motionless before the gravestone for a time. "Well, my dear, little Elizabeth is going to get married. I know you will be pleased. She has turned out to be a fine young woman, and the young man, Captain Frederick Harrington has a promising career. I only wish you were here to help me celebrate their marriage. It's hard to do things like this without you. I'm going to give Elizabeth one of your mother's necklaces which we brought along. I think I should give her the pearls, don't you? I hope you approve, my darling. Sleep well," Leonora said.

After standing motionless for a time, she returned home. The house was quiet so she looked in on all of the children but watched Elizabeth a little longer. "Sleep well, my darling. You'll have many busy days ahead," she said softly.

By the fall of the year all the plans had been completed for an early wedding in spring 1866. Elizabeth and Leonora consulted with many friends about what type of wedding dress she should have. They decided on a satin gown with many small, white bows all over the skirt. By January Leonora had finished sewing dresses for Elizabeth and Melanie, as well as a pale green dress for herself.

Melanie would be maid of honor for her sister, Karl would be the ringbearer and Heinrich, one of Frederick's brothers, would be the best man. On the day of the wedding the church was decorated with local flowers, but especially fleur de lis gathered from the surrounding woods. Vows were exchanged and toasts made at the modest reception Leonora had arranged for the young couple. Frederick hired a carriage so that they could drive off to Milwaukee about 25 miles away for their first evening together at the Hotel Baumgarten.

After they had departed, Melanie said to her mother, "I hope I will be able to find someone as good as Frederick for a husband. I don't know very many young men of that type."

"No need to rush, Melanie. You will find someone, I'm sure. Now after all, you're only 18, and there's plenty of time," Leonora said.

CHAPTER 19

Post-War Life In Wisconsin

"Karl, I declare, you grow more like your father every day," Leonora said one afternoon as she watched her 17 year old son making sketches of some farm animals. "If you don't have your nose in a book, you have a pencil in your hand."

"Oh, Mama, there are so many things to learn, but sometimes I get tired of reading, and then I've got to draw. I'm not very good at it, but it teaches me a lot about what's going on. The other day in school Mr. Handmacher said that he was sure General Grant would be the next president. He said some people called him a butcher because of the way he finished up the war. He said Grant would put the fear of God into some of the members of Congress and perhaps some things would get done in Washington," Karl said.

"I'm sure I wouldn't know about General Grant or anyone else for that matter. I guess all I can see is that people are going to push for more and more settlement of the West. Even in the short time we've lived in America you can see the push to keep moving. They get attracted to gold and silver mines in Nevada and Colorado. I guess some people get rich, but a lot of them seem to stay about as poor as they ever were," Leonora said.

"Do any people get rich around here, Mama?" Karl asked.

"Oh some do, I suppose. Some of the New York people come out to places like Chicago and seem to get rich. New railroads keep opening up, going into Minnesota and beyond. Some of those people like Mr. Jay Gould and Mr. Kim Fisk seem to make a lot of money. Why the interest in money? Are you planning on being rich?" Leonora asked.

"I guess it'd be nice to have a lot of money. How was it when you and father had a lot of money?" Karl asked.

"My dear, that seems like so long ago, I can hardly remember," Leonora said.

"What was it like? You lived in a big house and had lots of servants, didn't you?" Karl asked.

"Yes, I guess we did, but I'm not sure we were rich, not like some of the people who own railroads and steamship lines. They are very rich. Your father inherited a lot of property when he was quite young, and he thought it should be carefully guarded so his children would enjoy the same things. Of course, things didn't work out that way, and we had to leave almost everything behind. Your father and the ruling Prince where we lived disagreed on how the forests were to be managed. The Prince wanted to sell off large tracts of forests for construction purposes, but your father pointed out that once the trees were gone, there was no way to replenish them. The same thing is going to happen here if people don't learn you should only take some of the lumber out of a forest and not all of it. People are beginning to cut off much of the forest around Lake Superior in the same way they did in Germany and France. It'll be too bad if it comes to that," Leonora said.

"Did you like living in a big house, Mama?" Karl asked.

"Yes, in some ways it was very pleasant. Each of you could have had your own room, and your father could have his prized library all to himself," Leonora said.

"Did he have the grandfather's clock in his library?"

"Yes, he did. He loved it."

"Where was it made, and how old is it?" Karl asked.

"It was made somewhere in the Black Forest, not far from Freiburg. I think it was about 100 years old when your grandfather bought it. He had it before your father. One day you will have it," Leonora said.

"Not any time soon I won't. I don't even have a house," Karl said and then laughed as he declared this truism.

"There's so much to learn and no way to learn all of the things I'd like. One of these days I'll need to get a job," Karl said.

"Yes, that's so. You must think about all the possibilities. Lately I've been wondering about selling this place and moving to Michilac. I think there would be more opportunities for you and Melanie there. I've checked some on prices, and just now farm land is selling at a good price. What do you think of my idea?" Leonora asked.

"I like that idea. Of all the things one can do, straight farming interests me least of all. What does Melanie think?" Karl asked.

"I haven't discussed that matter with her but perhaps tonight would be a good time," Leonora said.

After discussing the issues with her children, Leonora decided to sell the farm and move to Michilac. A small house close to the lake became available, and in 1869 they moved there. By then both Melanie and Karl had finished high school.

Although they knew some people from Michilac, Melanie and Karl lost no time making new friends, some from the German Reformed Church and, for Karl, some from his job in a store which sold paint and other household products.

A young merchant from town, Tobias Augustus, began paying his respects to Melanie. The courtship continued for the better part of a year, and shortly after Easter 1870, Tobias asked her to marry him. After discussing the offer with her mother, she accepted. This wedding was more elaborate than Elizabeth's had been because this seemed to be the practice in the city.

The actual wedding was timed so that Elizabeth and Frederick could participate in the ceremony. Frederick was being reassigned to Ft. Crook in Minnesota, but he had some leave time to take which coincided with Melanie's wedding plans. Frederick had been promoted to Major in the interim since their marriage. They had two young children to bring along with them. After a short trip to Chicago, Tobias and Melanie settled in Michilac. In time they had four children.

Karl was able to combine some of his interests by becoming a fancy sign painter. This skill carried over to his interest in drawing and painting a wide variety of subjects, including some portraits an area becoming increasingly popular among the more affluent citizens. One of his subjects was Rosamunde Weikel, the daughter of a local prosperous merchant.

Karl dressed in the latest fashion, complete with a heavy velvet cravat. His hair, naturally curly, was worn long, and he had grown a handsome mustache. Rosa, as she was generally called, found him to be attractive though her parents thought his business ventures were rather modest. Despite the lukewarm reception he received from the Weikel family, Karl persisted.

He went to Milwaukee to attend a business school, a move that pleased Rosa's father greatly. During his absence he wrote, long, impassioned letters to his beloved. In time Karl won over both Rosa and her family.

"Karl, now that you are getting so serious about Rosamunde, you must think about some place to live. I have a suggestion I want you to think about," Leonora said.

"I can't imagine what you have in mind, Mama, so tell me," Karl said.

"I want to deed the house to you, and simply said, live with you rather than you with me. Does that sound attractive to you?" Leonora said.

"Mama, you never cease to amaze me. Of course, it sounds attractive, but you take me by surprise. Do you mind if I discuss this with Rosamunde?"

"No, of course not," Leonora said.

Almost at once Karl did discuss this proposition with Rosa. "Rosa, I must tell you about an interesting thing that happened just two days ago," Karl said one Sunday afternoon.

"What can it be? Tell me more," Rosa said. "What can it be? Tell me more," Rosa said. "My mother proposes that I should be a home owner by deeding her house to me, although she will retain a room for the rest of her days. Does that seem interesting?" Karl asked.

"Why, yes, it does. You know, Papa has felt that if I am to marry you, you should have a more substantial station than he thinks you have now. I'm sure he would like that arrangement very much. Will you talk to him about that?" Rosamunde said.

"Yes, but first, will you marry me, my dearest?" Karl said, getting down on his knees.

"Of course, I accept, silly. You always knew I would. Oh, I hope Papa agrees with all of this. Karl, do talk to him as soon as you can. I want nothing more than to be your devoted wife," Rosamunde said.

The very next night Karl spoke to Mr. Weikel. "Sir, I have come to you to seek your approval of my request to marry Rosamunde. I have taken the liberty of speaking with her, and she says she will consent," Karl said.

"Karl, I know Rosamunde is fond of you and we are too, but your business and personal situation is limited, would you not agree?" Mr. Weikel said.

"I'm not offended at what you say, but let me tell you

that my mother has proposed that she deed her house to me in anticipation of marriage," Karl said.

"Really? That is a most generous offer on her part. I presume she would live on there with you," Mr. Weikel asked.

"Yes, that is the arrangement. What do you think?" Karl said.

"Karl, I am pleased to agree to this marriage. In fact, I think it would be fine if you would help me in my business as well, once you and Rosamunde marry. How does that sound to you?" Mr. Weikel said.

"I accept. That is most kind of you, and I'm sure that would please Rosamunde very much," Karl said.

Karl left the presence of his rather somber father-in-law to-be and literally ran to Rosamunde's house to tell her of the talk with her father. Somewhat breathlessly he said, "Rosa, I am absolutely bowled over by your father!"

"Oh, Karl, what on earth could he have said to you to make you so breathless?" Rosamunde said.

"First, my love, I asked for your hand, and he sputtered until I told him my mother will deed over our house to me when I marry," he said.

"Yes, and then what?" she said.

"He said, 'yes' and then went on to say he wanted me to join him in his business down on Main Street. Can you imagine?" Karl said.

"What? Why that's almost beyond belief, but what did you say?"

"What did I say? Why, of course," I said, "With all my heart. But that's not all. He then asked me if we would accept some of the furniture which he has from a defunct inn in South Carolina. Again I said 'yes.' Do you think that was the right thing to say?" Karl said.

Rosamunde fairly jumped into his arms, saying, "Of course, my dearest. Oh, surely Heaven shines upon us! Will your mother continue to live in the house after we are married?" Rosamunde asked.

"Yes, that was part of the bargain. She will retain the front room for as long as she lives," Karl said.

"Then she can help mind any children we might have," Rosamunde said.

In June 1875 Rosamunde and Karl were married by Pastor Niemueller in the German reformed Church which both of them attended. It was a lovely day with abundant sunshine. The numerous bouquets of flowers made the church appear like a florist's shop. Later in the day there was a reception at the home of the Weikels. Both Karl and Rosamunde were radiant. On this special day all eyes were on them.

Tante Flora said to Tante Frieda, "I hear that old Heinrich has offered to take him into the business and then will give him some furniture as well."

"Oh, you don't say. My he's such a handsome young man. Leonora has offered them her house. Quite a good beginning for a couple who are so young," Tante Frieda replied.

Returning from their honeymoon at a small resort nearby, Karl and Rosamunde set out to move into their new house. The mahogany furniture had already been moved in, complete with a bed, dresser, dining room table and chairs, and many other accouterments. In time two daughters, Maria and Charlotte, and a son, Roland, were born.

Sitting together one evening, Rosamunde asked Leonora, "Do you ever have any regrets about having left Germany and your way of life over there?"

"There were times when I did, especially in the early years, but I had my family, and in the end that was all that mattered. I am truly the happiest when I am surrounded by my family," Leonora said.

Leonora continued to live with the young couple 16 years, until her death in 1891.

During the time that Karl and Rosamunde and their family were prospering, Max succeeded as owner of a small dry goods store. He and his family, consisting of his wife and their two children, were active in many ways in their community.

Over the years, and despite the distance from Germany, Leonora maintained contact with Magdalene through letters. Magdalene would pass along information about some of the others who remained in Europe. Gustav, one of Eduard's children had settled in Budapest and his large family prospered there. Heinrich, Rudolph's older half-brother, continued his work in various universities. He never married. Rudolph's older half-sister, Bertha married a young nobleman, Graf Weintraub, from Austria. They had six children.

All of these contacts ended with Magdalene's death in 1870.